"" Bain asked.

"Who are you?"

"My name's Clint Adams," Clint said.

"Adams?" Bain asked. "The Gunsmith?"

"That's right. Didn't plan on that, did you?" Clint asked.

"Just drop your gun and get out of the way," Bain said.

"If I drop my gun you'll kill me, because if you leave me alive I'll come after you."

"I'll bet I can draw and fire before you can pull the trigger."

"You want to bet your life?"

DON'T MISS THESE
ALL-ACTION WESTERN SERIES
FROM THE BERKLEY PUBLISHING GROUP

THE GUNSMITH by J. R. Roberts

Clint Adams was a legend among lawmen, outlaws, and ladies. They called him . . . the Gunsmith.

LONGARM by Tabor Evans

The popular long-running series about Deputy U.S. Marshal Custis Long—his life, his loves, his fight for justice.

SLOCUM by Jake Logan

Today's longest-running action Western. John Slocum rides a deadly trail of hot blood and cold steel.

BUSHWHACKERS by B. J. Lanagan

An action-packed series by the creators of Longarm! The rousing adventures of the most brutal gang of cutthroats ever assembled—Quantrill's Raiders.

DIAMONDBACK by Guy Brewer

Dex Yancey is Diamondback, a Southern gentleman turned con man when his brother cheats him out of the family fortune. Ladies love him. Gamblers hate him. But nobody pulls one over on Dex . . .

WILDGUN by Jack Hanson

The blazing adventures of mountain man Will Barlow—from the creators of Longarm!

TEXAS TRACKER by Tom Calhoun

J.T. Law: the most relentless—and dangerous—manhunter in all Texas. Where sheriffs and posses fail, he's the best man to bring in the most vicious outlaws—for a price.

THE GUNSMITH

345

SOMEONE ELSE'S TROUBLE

J. R. ROBERTS

JOVE BOOKS, NEW YORK

THE BERKLEY PUBLISHING GROUP
Published by the Penguin Group
Penguin Group (USA) Inc.
375 Hudson Street, New York, New York 10014, USA
Penguin Group (Canada), 90 Eglinton Avenue East, Suite 700, Toronto, Ontario M4P 2Y3, Canada
(a division of Pearson Penguin Canada Inc.)
Penguin Books Ltd., 80 Strand, London WC2R 0RL, England
Penguin Group Ireland, 25 St. Stephen's Green, Dublin 2, Ireland (a division of Penguin Books Ltd.)
Penguin Group (Australia), 250 Camberwell Road, Camberwell, Victoria 3124, Australia
(a division of Pearson Australia Group Pty. Ltd.)
Penguin Books India Pvt. Ltd., 11 Community Centre, Panchsheel Park, New Delhi—110 017, India
Penguin Group (NZ), 67 Apollo Drive, Rosedale, North Shore 0632, New Zealand
(a division of Pearson New Zealand Ltd.)
Penguin Books (South Africa) (Pty.) Ltd., 24 Sturdee Avenue, Rosebank, Johannesburg 2196,
South Africa

Penguin Books Ltd., Registered Offices: 80 Strand, London WC2R 0RL, England

This is a work of fiction. Names, characters, places, and incidents either are the product of the author's imagination or are used fictitiously, and any resemblance to actual persons, living or dead, business establishments, events, or locales is entirely coincidental.

SOMEONE ELSE'S TROUBLE

A Jove Book / published by arrangement with the author

PRINTING HISTORY
Jove edition / September 2010

ISBN: 978-0-515-14839-8

JOVE®
Jove Books are published by The Berkley Publishing Group,
a division of Penguin Group (USA) Inc.,
375 Hudson Street, New York, New York 10014.
JOVE® is a registered trademark of Penguin Group (USA) Inc.
The "J" design is a trademark of Penguin Group (USA) Inc.

PRINTED IN THE UNITED STATES OF AMERICA

10 9 8 7 6 5 4 3 2 1

ONE

The job had to go off without a hitch.

But that meant different things to different people.

To Noah Bain, that meant having none of his people get killed.

To Travis Bledsoe—one of Bain's men—that meant not getting any blood on his clothes.

Bain looked at Bledsoe. He knew that their thinking didn't always run concurrent. But that's why they were a good team. Bledsoe usually let Bain do the thinking for both of them.

They were on a bluff, looking down at one of the largest ranches in West Texas. Donald Connelly raised horses, the finest in any part of the state. He had a reputation for not only owning one of the largest spreads, but working it, as well. At the moment he was out with his men, rounding up his herd for a sale to the army. There was only a skeleton crew left at the ranch—a cook, a couple of ranch hands, and Connelly's family.

"Okay," Bain said, "Take 'em in."

"Right."

Bain put his hand on Bledsoe's arm.

"You know what I want," he said.

"I know."

"Don't make a mess."

Bledsoe smiled.

"You know me, Noah."

"Yeah, I do," Bain said, "that's why I'm tellin' you not to make a mess."

Bledsoe nodded. He walked over to where the rest of the men were waiting—six men on horseback, all well trained and well armed.

"The boss wants us to be neat," he said as he mounted up.

"Yeah," Owney Roundtree said with a big grin, "like always."

"Let's go," Bledsoe said.

Since the injury to his leg, Brad Trainer never went out on the range with the men. He walked with a heavy limp, and riding a horse for more than ten minutes caused him a lot of pain. But he had worked for Donald Connelly for more than twenty years, so there was no way Connelly was going to let him go. So Trainer was always around the ranch, doing whatever odd jobs he could handle with his bad leg the way it was.

It was Trainer who saw the seven men riding down the hill toward the ranch. He didn't carry a gun, and he couldn't run, so he turned and started dragging his bad leg toward the house as fast as he could. He wanted to warn them and started shouting, hoping they or Eddie Castro, the other hand, would hear him.

"Hey! Hey! Trouble comin'! Hey, the house! Eddie, where are ya?"

Now, he didn't really know whether or not the seven

men meant trouble, but he'd been around for a long time, and he generally knew when somebody was carrying bad news with them.

These boys carried bad news like a second skin.

Emma Leslie, the cook, had worked for the Connelly family for seven years. She entered the kitchen at five a.m. every morning and rarely left it until after dinner was served. She was standing at the sink in front of the window when she heard somebody shouting. The kitchen was on the side of the house, not the back, or she never would have heard it. She craned her neck to look out the window and saw poor Trainer hurrying toward the house, dragging his bad leg.

Something was wrong.

"Mrs. Connelly!" she shouted.

Beth Connelly had been married to Donald for more than twenty-five years, had stood by him through good and bad. She had been spattered with both his seat and his blood, and she had fought alongside him. When she heard Emma shout, she recognized the panic in the woman's voice, so she grabbed for the nearest gun, a Winchester hanging on pegs on the wall of the living room.

She took it to the front door with her.

TWO

Bledsoe led the six men to the ranch house, saw the man running toward the house—or trying to run. He was dragging one leg behind him, as if it was of no use to him. Bledsoe rode up on the man and put a bullet into his spine. Now none of his limbs were of any use to him.

Beth Connelly opened the front door just in time to see poor Trainer gunned down from behind. She caught her breath, then released it and shouted, "Emma!"

She raised the rifle and fired one shot at the approaching men.

At the sound of the first shot from the house, all seven men drew their guns and began to fire. The figure in the doorway dropped the rifle and began to dance in place as chunks of lead acted as if they were the strings and she was the puppet.

* * *

Emma came running from the kitchen just in time to see Mrs. Connelly's body jerk and dance as bullets rained down upon her.

She screamed.

Bledsoe did not slow his approach. He rode up the front steps of the house and right through the front door, trampling the dead woman's body, which lay in the doorway. Several of the men rode in with him while the others stayed outside to provide cover.

Bledsoe saw the older woman wearing an apron. She was standing there with her hands over her mouth, her eyes wide with fear. He pumped two slugs into her. Her apron blossomed with red and the fear left her eyes. In fact, everything left her eyes and she slumped to the floor.

"I'm gonna look for it," Bledsoe said. "The rest of the house is yours."

The men whooped and hollered and began riding through the house, looking for anything of value.

Bledsoe rode his horse throughout the first floor. It wasn't until he went down a long hallway that he found what the rancher must have used as his office. What he was looking for was hanging on pegs on the wall. He rode the horse up to it, plucked it, and tied it to his saddle. Then he turned the horse and rode back out to the front of the house.

The men had ransacked the house, taken anything that looked valuable—silverware, candleholders, weapons, some cash.

"Hey, Bledsoe," one of them called. "Look what I found."

Bledsoe turned and saw Roundtree holding a girl in her early twenties.

"Where was she?"

"Hiding upstairs."

"Anybody else up there?"

"No."

Bledsoe looked at the girl again. She stared at him with eyes that were filled with hate and pain, but no fear.

She was the most beautiful thing he had ever seen.

"Should I kill 'er?" Roundtree asked. He took out his knife and held it to her neck from behind. Bledsoe still didn't see any fear in her eyes.

"No," he said, "put the knife away."

Roundtree looked disappointed. All the men knew he'd rather kill a woman than fuck her. It made him scary and dangerous.

"Put the knife away and tie her up," Bledsoe said. "She's comin' with us."

Roundtree shrugged.

"You're the boss."

Bledsoe looked at the rest of the men.

"I got what we came for," he said. "Let's go." Then he looked at Roundtree again. "Put her up here, on my horse."

Bledsoe took her as Roundtree lifted her and placed her in front of him. She didn't struggle at all. Maybe, he thought, she actually wanted to go with him.

Elizabeth Connelly knew her mother was dead; she saw her lying in the doorway. Shot, and trampled over by horses. From that point on she felt no fear, and she didn't struggle. She wanted the men to take her with them, because at her earliest opportunity she was going to kill them.

All of them.

* * *

As the seven men rode away with Elizabeth Connelly and anything of value they could take, Eddie Castro came out of the barn. He ran to the house, found both Beth Connelly and the cook dead. He came back out and watched from the porch as the seven men disappeared over a rise.

He'd hidden in the barn—not because he was afraid, but because he knew somebody had to stay alive to tell Donald Connelly what had happened. His boss had to know who had killed his wife and kidnapped his daughter.

THREE

Clint Adams rode into the West Texas town of Chandlerville, knowing he was riding smack into the middle of someone else's trouble—again. But he had no choice. This time, the summons had come from a very old and very good friend, and it had been urgent. So urgent it had tracked him down to Louisiana, where he had been playing some very important hands of poker. But he'd dropped all that and responded immediately.

A matter of days, but he hoped not too many days.

He stopped at the Chandler Hotel, tied Eclipse off outside, and entered the lobby. He knew that the town and the hotel were named for Philip Chandler, who had founded the town many years ago. Chandler had died nearly twenty years ago, but the town still bore his name.

These days, the biggest name in town was Donald Connelly, who had the biggest spread in West Texas just outside of town. Clint knew if Connelly wanted to he could change the name of the town, but he wasn't that kind of man.

Clint presented himself at the front desk; when he told the clerk his name, the man came to attention.

"Yes, sir, your room is ready, but Mr. Connelly would like you to meet him in the Cattleman's Club as soon as you arrive."

"That's fine," Clint said. "Just give me the key and take these upstairs." He dropped his saddlebags and rifle on the desk.

"And your horse? Shall I have someone take care of it?"

"Only if you have someone who knows horses," Clint said, "otherwise he'll lose a finger."

"I have just the man, sir."

"Fine. Thanks. Where's the Cattleman's Club? Same place as always?"

The clerk looked surprised that Clint had been to the establishment before.

"Yes, sir, same place."

Clint nodded and left the hotel. He turned left, walked two blocks, and stopped in front of the Cattleman's Club. He took a moment to remove his hat and use it to try to slap as much dust from his clothes as he could before entering. He was immediately stopped by a thirtyish man in a black suit, because this was a private club.

"Sir?"

"Clint Adams for Mr. Connelly," Clint said.

"Yes, sir!" the man said, immediately snapping to attention. "This way."

He led Clint through the club, past men who gave him scathing looks because of the condition of his clothes. Just to be ornery, Clint kept slapping dust from himself all the way.

The man led him to a small private back room and opened the door.

"Go right in, sir."

Clint entered, saw four men standing around a table. They all looked up at him. He saw three things: the badge on one man's chest, the army uniform on another, and the haunted look in Donald Connelly's eyes.

"Clint, thank God," Connelly said.

He rushed across the room to grab Clint's hand.

"Thanks for coming so quickly," Connelly's said.

"What's it about, Don?"

"They killed Beth, Clint," Connelly said. "Killed my wife, and took Elizabeth."

"Elizabeth," Clint said.

"My daughter."

"I know," Clint said, remembering a small girl he had bounced on his knee. "She must be—how old?"

"Twenty-two," Connelly said. "Just turned twenty-two."

Clint knew Connelly was in his late fifties, but the man seemed to be carrying many more years than that on his shoulders, and in his eyes.

"When?" Clint asked.

"Three days ago," the man with the badge said. He came up behind Connelly. "Sheriff Potts, Mr. Adams."

The two men shook hands.

"We have a map over here."

Clint walked to the table with Connelly and Potts, even though he didn't need a map to see Texas. It was in his head.

"We tracked them to here," Potts said, "and lost the trail."

"What?" Clint asked.

"We know this bunch," Potts said. "They hit and run; have done it all over Texas. But this time they wanted something in particular, according to Mr. Connelly."

"What was it, Donny?" Clint asked.

"A sword, Clint."

"A sword?" Clint asked. "A saber?"

"No," Connelly said, "a samurai sword."

"What the heck were you doing with a samurai sword?" Clint asked

"It was supposed to be a gift," Connelly said.

"For you or from you?"

"From the United States government, Mr. Adams," the soldier said. "I'm Captain Mundy."

"Captain." They shook hands. "You must have men who can track these bastards."

"The army is here as a courtesy, Mr. Adams," Mundy said. "We can't get involved on an official level."

"Why not?" Clint asked.

"Well, Mr. Connelly has arranged for a visit by a member of the Japanese government, a Mr. Tanaka. That visit was not sanctioned by the government."

Clint had recently had another brush with the United States government, had come out of that not liking them very much. This situation was not going to improve his feelings. He turned and looked at his friend.

"Donny, you look like you could use something to eat," he said. "I know I could."

"But Clint—"

"I'm sure the sheriff and the captain can do without you for an hour."

He was giving Connelly a hard look, trying to send a message. The man finally seemed to get it.

"Well, all right," Connelly said. "I suppose I could choke something down."

Clint turned to the other men. He still hadn't been introduced to the third one.

"See you gents in an hour or so?" he asked.

"Of course," the captain said, and the sheriff nodded.

Clint put his arm around Connelly's shoulder.

"Everybody's got to eat, right, Donny?" he asked, leading his friend to the door.

"I suppose."

"You'll feel a lot better after we've had something to eat," Clint said. "A lot better."

FOUR

As they left the room Connelly said, "We can go to my table in the dining—"

"No," Clint said, "let's get out of here. I want to talk where there's no chance of being overheard."

"B-but why?"

"I don't want the army overhearing us. Or the sheriff," Clint said.

"But Clint—"

"And I really am hungry. Take me someplace for a good steak."

"We have the best steaks here—"

"Donny!" Clint said, shaking his friend. "Just do it, okay? You want my help?"

"Well, of course—"

"Then you're going to have to trust me," Clint said. "Can you do that?"

"Of course."

"Good," Clint said, "then take me to a steak."

* * *

"When did he send for Clint Adams?" Captain Mundy asked the sheriff as soon as Clint left the room with Donald Connelly.

"I didn't know he had," Sheriff Potts said. "I guess they're old friends."

"You didn't know that?" Mundy asked. "How long have you known Connelly?"

"Seven years," Potts said. "That's when I got hired as sheriff."

Mundy looked at the other man in the room, who had not been introduced to Clint.

"What about having the Gunsmith involved in this?" he asked.

"I still have my man coming in later today," the man said. "If they can work together, then why not?"

"When is Mr. Tanaka getting here?"

"In a week," the other man said.

"So we have a week to get it back," Mundy said.

"And a week to get Mr. Connelly's daughter back," the sheriff reminded him.

"Yes," Mundy said, "and the girl."

Connelly took Clint to a steak house two blocks from the Cattleman's Club. When they were seated, Clint ordered for both of them, because Connelly was obviously not interested in food.

"Go ahead," Clint said, "tell me what's going on. What's this about a samurai sword?"

"Akemi Tanaka is a former feudal lord of Japan, a Daimyo, but since the changes in Japan he had to return all his holdings to the emperor. Part of those holdings was the sword, which was stolen from my house three days ago."

"How did you get it?"

"I bought it in San Francisco."

"What's so special about it?"

"It once belonged to Ii Naomasa, a lord from the fifteen hundreds. It was made by Rai Kunimitsuand; it may have been the last sword he made in thirteen fifty."

"How do you know all of this?"

"I got interested in Japanese swords a few years ago," he said. "Bought that one in San Francisco, as I said. But I don't care about the sword, I care about my daughter."

"And the army?"

"They apparently care about the sword—unofficially."

"So they're not helping?"

"In a sense," Connelly said. He cut a piece of steak and put it in his mouth. Then did the same with a second piece.

"What do you mean, in a sense?"

"The captain brought that other man with him."

"The other man?"

"The one you didn't meet," Connelly said. "He's a representative of the government."

"Well, if that's the case then I still don't want to meet him," Clint said. "What's his contribution to this?"

"He has another man coming in later today who is supposed to be helpful. He trusts that man, and I trust you. Maybe the two of you can work together."

"Maybe," Clint said. "I assume you brought me here to get your daughter back?"

"Yes," Connelly said.

"And the sword?"

"I don't care about the sword," he said. "They can keep it. I want Elizabeth."

"All right, then," Clint said. "Tell me what happened, and tell me about the men who did it."

FIVE

Connelly told Clint how the sword had been stolen along with everything else in the house that might have had some value—and his daughter.

"They shot Beth down, then rode over here, trampling her body," he said. He'd stopped eating. "And the cook, they shot her, too. And one of my men, a poor cripple I kept around because he'd been with me for so long."

"Did anyone survive?"

"Yes, one of my men, Eddie Castro. He's the one who told us it was seven men, led by a big man riding a huge bay."

"How did he survive?"

"He hid, felt guilty about it until I told him he'd done the right thing. It's the only reason we know anything about what happened."

"And you know who they were?"

"I don't, but the army seems to think they do."

"Then I guess I'll have to talk with Captain Mundy again," Clint said, making a face.

"I'll make sure you do."

"I'll need to talk to your man," Clint said.

"Of course."

"Away from the army and the government man. Is he with the Secret Service?"

"I don't think so," Connelly said. "I don't see any reason why the Secret Service would be involved."

"Good," Clint said. "I've about had my fill of them."

Connelly tried to eat another bite, but he dropped the fork onto the table. He watched while Clint finished his meal.

"Can we get back now?" Connelly said.

"Set me up with your man Castro, and then you can go back."

"Don't you want to look at their map?"

"I don't need a map," Clint said. "I'll just need someone to take me to the point where you lost the trail."

"That won't be a problem," Connelly said.

As they walked out of the restaurant, Connelly said, "Castro is in town. I'll put you together with him."

"Good. If the sheriff and captain ask you where I am tell them I'm checking into the hotel."

"Okay," Connelly said, "but why the secrecy?"

"Mundy and the government man are not going to look out for your interests, Donny," Clint said. "I am."

"And the sheriff?"

"I don't know," Clint said. "You tell me. What's your relationship with him?"

"We get along well," Connelly said.

"Do you think I should talk to him alone, too?" Clint asked.

"You'll probably better make up your own mind about him if you do. And he's probably going to have to be the one to take you out there. And in the end, I think he still wants to take out a posse."

"Okay, I'll talk to him, too."

"Castro's in the same hotel as you," Connelly said. "Tell him I sent you."

"Okay," Clint said. "Arrange for me to talk with the captain without his government man."

"I'll do my best."

"I'll catch up to you later. Where are you staying? At the ranch?"

"No," Connelly said. "I ain't going out there. I'll be at the club."

"Okay," Clint said.

"Clint, I'm really glad you're here—but you gotta get out there as soon as possible."

"Tomorrow," Clint said. "I'll start tomorrow. I promise."

SIX

Clint was only too happy to help Donald Connelly to get his daughter back, he was just sorry he had to deal with the government to do it.

He went to his hotel, saw that Eclipse had been moved from in front of it.

"Where's my horse?" he asked the clerk.

"We have a stable right out back," the clerk said. "He's there, and bein' well taken care of."

"Okay, I'll check on him. What room is Eddie Castro in?"

"Mr. Castro is in room five."

"Is he there now?"

"I believe he's across the street at the saloon."

"Thanks. Oh, how will I know him?"

"He's very young. I mean, he looks eighteen, but he's old enough to drink."

"Okay, thanks."

Clint went directly to the saloon across the street. It was small, had only a few men in it, and Eddie Castro was standing at the bar, leaning over a beer.

"Are you Castro?" Clint asked.

"That's right."

"Your boss sent me to talk to you," Clint said. "I'm Clint Adams."

"For real?" Castro asked, straightening up. "You're the Gunsmith? He really does know you?"

Clint smiled.

"Yeah, he really does. Can I buy you another beer?"

"Sure."

"Let's move to a table," Clint said. "I need you to tell me all about what happened."

"Are you gonna get Elizabeth back?"

"I'm going to try."

"Okay," Castro said, "I'll tell you everything I saw."

They moved to a table.

When Clint finished with Castro, he thanked the man.

"No problem," Castro said. "Do you know when the boss is gonna go back to the ranch?"

"No, I don't," Clint said. "But I think he'll probably send you back soon."

"Don't know if I wanna go back," Castro said. "I'm kinda ashamed."

"For what?"

"For hiding," the younger man said. "For not tryin' to help."

"If you had, you'd be dead, too," Clint said, "and we'd have nothing to go on. You've been a big help, Eddie."

"Really? Thanks."

They stood up from the table.

"Mr. Adams?"

"Yes?"

"Do you think when you go after Elizabeth I could go, too?"

Clint almost said no immediately, but he decided to go easy, so he said, "I don't know, Eddie. We'll have to see. Okay?"

"Sure," Castro said. "Okay."

Clint left Castro at the saloon and returned to the hotel. He walked through to the back and checked on Eclipse in the stable. The big horse seemed content, as if he'd been well rubbed down and well fed.

"Beautiful animal," the liveryman said. "I'll take good care of him."

"I know you will," Clint said. "Thanks."

Clint left the livery, went back into the hotel and up to his room. He used the pitcher and basin to wash as well as he could, and then changed his clothes so he'd stop dropping trail dust all over town.

He needed to talk to the sheriff and the captain, separate from each other, and he needed to talk to both of them away from the government man. But only Connelly could arrange that. He was going to have to go back to the Cattleman's Club so Connelly could arrange it.

He strapped on his gun, left the hotel, and walked over to the Cattleman's.

SEVEN

Clint was greeted by the same man when he stepped into the Cattleman's Club.

"Mr. Connelly again, sir?"

"Yes," Clint said, "but please ask him to meet me out here, instead."

"All right, sir."

Clint waited where he was until the man returned with Don Connelly.

"They still back there, looking at their map?" Clint asked.

"The captain and the other man—his name's Drake, by the way—they're still there."

"Where's the sheriff?"

"In his office."

"Good, I'll go and talk to him there."

"When do you want to talk to the captain?"

"How about an hour from now?"

"Where?" Connelly asked.

"Away from Drake."

"I own a store in town," Connelly said. "It's closed

down now, but I still have the building." He took a key from his pocket and told Clint where the building was. "Be there in an hour."

"How will he get in?" Clint asked.

"I have another key."

"Okay."

"Are you sure you don't want to talk to Drake?" Connelly asked.

"I'm very sure," Clint said.

"Okay, then," Connelly said. "I'll keep him occupied."

"Good. After I've talked with the captain, I'll meet you at my hotel, in my room."

"All right."

Clint nodded and left the Cattleman's Club.

He knocked on the door of the sheriff's office before entering. Sheriff Potts looked up from his desk with a frown that disappeared when he recognized Clint.

"Mr. Adams," he said. "Have a seat. Sorry I can't offer you any coffee, but the pot's gone cold."

"That's okay, Sheriff," Clint said. He pulled a chair up in front of the man's desk and sat.

"Can I help you with somethin'?"

"I need some information on who killed Beth Connelly and kidnapped Elizabeth."

"And stole the sword."

"I don't care about the sword," Clint said.

"Captain Mundy and Mr. Drake do."

"Then let them worry about getting it back," Clint said. "I'm concerned with bringing back Beth's killer, and returning Elizabeth to her father."

"Well," the Sheriff said, "guess I can't blame you for that. What do ya need to know?"

"Well, first," Clint said, "who were these men? You

said you knew this bunch, that they've been active for a while."

"They're run by a fella named Noah Bain, but it's Travis Bledsoe who actually carries out the jobs, and he's a bloodthirsty sonofabitch."

"Kills for fun?"

"Oh, yeah."

"So why didn't he kill Elizabeth?"

"When did you last see Elizabeth?" Potts asked.

"Not for a long time, since she was a little girl."

"Well, she ain't a little girl anymore," Potts said. "She's beautiful—probably the most beautiful girl I've ever seen."

"So you think Bledsoe fell in love with her?" Clint asked.

"I think he saw the value of her."

"You think he's going to ransom her?"

"No, Mr. Adams," Potts said, "I think he and Bain will probably sell her."

Clint took that in for a moment. Potts opened a drawer and took out a bottle and two glasses.

"I don't have any coffee," he said, "but how about a drink?"

"Sure."

The lawman poured two glasses and pushed one over to Clint.

"Thanks. So what kind of posse did you take out with you?" Clint asked.

"Couple of deputies, some storekeepers," Potts said. "Tracked them as long as we could. Got back and found the army and Drake, here."

"Drake show you any identification?"

"No," Potts said. "Mundy vouched for him, but I don't really know who he works for."

"And Mundy has no men with him?"

Potts shook his head and said, "None."

"Were you planning on going out again?"

Potts nodded and said, "As soon as I got a decent posse together."

"Can you show me where you lost the trail?"

"Sure," Potts said, "but do you plan on ridin' out alone, or goin' with us?"

"I'm thinking I'll start out with you and then see what happens."

"Suits me," Potts said, raising his glass, "and glad to have you."

Clint raised his glass and drained it.

"You know anything about the sword and the man who's supposed to get it?"

"I don't know nothin' about no sword or no Japanese," Potts said. "I'm just a town sheriff. You'll have to talk to Captain Mundy for that."

"I plan on doing that."

"I gotta tell ya, I don't like the captain," Potts said. "If I was you I'd watch my back around him—and around that fella, Drake."

"He seems to be the joker in this deck," Clint said, and stood up. "When were you planning on riding out again?" he asked.

"First light," Potts said.

"How's your posse looking?"

"I'm leaving the storekeepers home this time," Potts said.

"Sounds like a good plan."

Clint walked to the door.

"Hey, Adams?"

Clint turned.

"Any chance I can deputize you for this?"

"No," Clint said, "I'm here for Connelly. I don't need a badge,"

"Okay," Potts said, "just thought I'd ask."

"See you in the morning, Sheriff."

EIGHT

Clint left the sheriff's office and followed the directions
Connelly had given him to the building he owned. It was
a one-story building with a lot of windows in front. An
outline of some letters above the door showed that the
building had last been a hardware store.

Clint tried the front door, found it unlocked, and
entered. It was empty, so he was apparently the first to
arrive. Of course, there was no guarantee the captain
would come. It would depend on how persuasive
Connelly could be, or how much influence he had.

Clint checked the storeroom in the back, found it
also empty. Checked the back door to make sure it was
locked, then went back to the front room. He heard
footsteps on the boardwalk outside, then the knob turned
and the door opened.

"Adams?" Mundy called, stepping inside.

"Here, Captain."

"What's this all about?" Mundy asked.

"Just wanted to have a private chat with you," Clint
said, "away from the sheriff, and Mr. Drake."

"Chat about what?"

"About why you and Mr. Drake are here."

"We're just trying to be helpful."

"And you want to get that sword back, right?"

"Look," Mundy said, taking off his hat to reveal unruly black hair that made him younger than Clint first figured, "I know you're friends with Connelly and you want to get his daughter back. But it's because he has you and the sheriff on his side that I can afford to think about the sword."

"What's so important about the sword?"

"We're just looking to avoid any kind of international incident. Mr. Tanaka represents the emperor of Japan."

"So the sword will go to the emperor?"

"As I understand it, yes."

"Okay," Clint said, "so that's why Drake is here, too?"

"Drake represents the president."

"Well, well," Clint said, "so we've got the president of the United States and the emperor of Japan involved in this."

"So you can understand why we're here."

"What I don't understand is why you're here without a troop of men."

"That's not your concern, sir," Mundy said. "I understand you'll be trying to track these men down. What kind of assistance can I give you, as far as information?"

"None," Clint said. "The sheriff told me who they are, and you've shown me who you and Mr. Drake are."

"What do you mean—"

"As usual," Clint said, cutting him off, "the government has its own agenda, which has nothing to do with helping anybody else. I don't require anything from you or from Drake. I'm done with you."

"There's no reason to get so—"

"What? Offended?"

"Adams, I know your reputation," Mundy said. "Don't get in the army's way."

"So you do have men out there hunting for the sword?" Clint asked.

"I didn't say that."

"That's right," Clint said. "You didn't." Clint headed for the door. "I'm done here."

"Okay, wait a minute," Mundy said. He put his hat back on.

"What?"

"Drake wants to talk to you."

"About what?"

"That's his business, I guess."

Clint laughed.

"So he's even keeping you in the dark?" Clint asked.

"I have my orders, Adams," Mundy said. "Will you talk with him?"

"Why not?" Clint asked. "I've talked to everyone else. Where?"

"The club is good enough."

"When?"

Mundy shrugged and said, "Now. I can escort you over there."

"*Escort* me?"

Mundy shrugged again.

"I'll just walk over there with you," he said, and then added, "if you don't mind."

"No, Captain," Clint said, opening the door, "I don't mind, at all."

NINE

Clint was surprised to find Drake waiting for him in the main room, with other members seated around him having their coffee or whiskey, discussing the events of the day.

Mundy walked Clint over to Drake, who said, "Thank you for coming, Mr. Adams. That'll be all, Captain."

Mundy stiffened at the dismissal, but turned and walked away.

"Have a seat?" Drake asked.

"You have a reason for treating him that way?" Clint asked, sitting opposite the man.

Drake looked at Clint and didn't smile when said, "Because I can."

"I don't think I like you very much, Mr. Drake," Clint said.

"That's fine with me, Mr. Adams," Drake said. "I'm not here for you to like."

"What are you here for, Mr. Drake?"

Drake sat back in his chair and crossed his legs. He

was a tall, slender man with neatly cut brown hair, wearing an expensive suit and a superior look.

"The president is very concerned for Mr. Connelly's daughter, and very sorry for the loss of his wife."

"So he sent you to convey his feelings to Connelly?" Clint asked.

"Well, I'm here to do a little more than that."

"Oh, yeah," Clint said, "the sword."

"I sent a telegram to Washington today, after you arrived," Clint said. "They seem to feel you might be our best bet to catch this gang."

"Really? I'm flattered."

"I don't agree, of course."

"Of course."

"I think these things should be left to the professionals."

"Like Sheriff Potts?"

"I was thinking more of myself," Drake said.

"So you're going to get on a horse and hunt them down?" Clint asked.

Drake made a face and said, "Hardly."

"Well then what makes you such a professional?" Clint asked.

"I have resources."

"Secret Service resources?"

"I'm not a great supporter of the Secret Service," Drake said.

"So you're talking about . . . what? Some new group you're forming?"

"You don't have the clearance for any of this, Adams," Drake said. "Suffice it to say I have plans for recovering that sword, and I don't want you getting in the way."

"Why does it matter who catches this gang and recovers the sword?" Clint asked. "Oh, and by the way, brings back a man's daughter and the men who killed his wife."

"Somehow," Drake said, "I don't believe you're in this just to help your friend. I think you've got an agenda of your own."

"That's because men like you—who always have an agenda—just can't believe that other people don't. You probably don't even know what the word *friendship* means, Drake."

"Spare me, Adams," Drake said. "Friendship is not an asset in my business."

"Well, Mr. Drake," Clint said, standing up, "since I'm not really going to need to worry about you out there, I don't see that we have anything more to say to one another."

"Sit back down," Drake said. "I haven't said you can go."

Clint had to laugh.

"Since when do I need your permission to leave, Drake?" Clint asked. "You've got me mixed up with Captain Mundy."

"I know your reputation in the West, Adams," Drake said. "A 'living legend,' huh? Well, I also know your reputation in Washington, D.C. You have no respect for authority, no respect for your betters."

"If I have any betters, Drake," Clint said, "I've never run into them in Washington, D.C."

"See, that's what I mean, right there."

Some of the other club members were now starting to notice what was going on. A few were looking for a waiter so they could complain, and others were simply trying to hear what was being said.

"You're a gunman, Adams," Drake said. "Where do you get off thinking you're better than anyone in Washington—"

"I don't have to think it when drones like you come out here to the West and prove it to me."

Drake stood up quickly, then, his jaw clenching.

"Come on, Drake," Clint invited. "Just give me a reason."

"You-you wouldn't dare shoot me, not in front of all these people."

"I wouldn't have to shoot you, Drake," Clint said, lowering his voice, "I'd just have to knock you through that wall."

Drake stared at Clint, then backed off.

"I know about your friendship with Jim West," Drake said. "It's worked well for you in the past, but it won't help you this time if you get in my way."

"I'm not going to need Jim West to take care of you, Drake."

"You wouldn't dare—"

Clint lashed out with a straight left that caught Drake flush on the nose, exploding it. He started to choke as the blood ran down into his mouth.

"You said that once too often," Clint told him.

TEN

Donald Connelly was standing in the lobby with Captain Mundy as Clint walked away, leaving behind a hacking, staggering Drake.

"What was that about?" Connelly asked.

"I'm not sure," Clint said. "He seemed to just be trying to make me mad."

"I guess he succeeded," Mundy asked.

Clint looked at the soldier.

"You better take him to a doctor, before he chokes to death on his own blood."

Mundy took a step toward Drake, then thought better of it.

"Maybe I'll have a drink first," he said, "to steady my nerves."

"Mundy, you may not be as bad as I first figured," Clint said.

"Don't count on it, Mr. Adams."

"Come on," Clint said, grabbing Connelly's arm and pulling him outside.

* * *

"You think that was smart?" Connelly asked.

"Probably not, but it felt good."

"What made you so mad?"

"Let's just say Mr. Drake was paying for somebody else's sins."

"Well, okay," Connelly said. "You've talked to the sheriff, the captain, and Drake. What's your next move?"

"In the morning I'll be riding out with Sherriff Potts and his posse," Clint said.

"Are you gonna track for them?"

"I'll ride with them at least to the point where Potts lost the trail. After that I might be better off riding alone."

"What about Drake's man?"

"When is he supposed to get here?"

"Today, I thought. Still might arrive."

"Do you know who he is?"

"No," Connelly said. "Haven't even heard a name."

"Okay, well, if he gets here in time he can join the posse."

"What if he wants to go out on his own?"

"That'll be up to him," Clint said. "Won't affect my decision one way or another." Clint poked his friend in the chest. "You look like you're going fall over. Why don't you get some sleep?"

"I've tried; I can't sleep."

"Get some rest, then," Clint said. "You're not going to do Elizabeth any good if you keel over."

"Yeah, okay."

"I'm going to my room."

"Turning in?"

"Not yet," Clint said. "I'll clean my guns, do some reading. Relax. It's like a ritual I go through before . . ."

"Before you go out hunting?"

"Donny—"

"Clint, I really appreciate you comin' so quick," Connelly said. "Did I tell you that?"

"Yeah, Donny, you told me," Clint said. "Go on, get some rest."

"I'll see you in the morning," Connelly said. "First light?"

"That's what the sheriff said."

"Okay, see you then."

Clint watched his friend walk away, a sad slump to his shoulders, then turned and walked to his hotel.

He stopped at the desk.

"Sir?" the clerk said, brightly.

"If anybody asks for me, I'm in my room," Clint said.

"Yes, sir."

Briefly, he considered going across the street to the small saloon for a drink, but then he decided against it. Instead, he went upstairs. He took off his gun belt, hung it on the bedpost, then sat on the bed and removed his boots for the first time in days. The socks he had on were done, and he tossed them aside. He had another pair in his saddlebags.

He looked down at his left hand, saw some of Drake's blood on his knuckles. He went to the dresser, poured some water into the basin, and washed the blood off. He might have to pay later for breaking Drake's nose, but for now it still felt good.

ELEVEN

After Clint left the club, Captain Mundy took Drake over to the doctor's office. The doctor straightened the man's nose, cleaned him off, and then bandaged him.

"Your eyes are already blackening," he told Drake. "It'll look worse in the morning. Don't worry about it. The bruises will fade . . . eventually."

Mundy walked Drake back to the club and up to his room. The man was still a bit unsteady on his feet when they reached the door.

"Come inside," Drake said.

"All right."

Mundy walked Drake to one of the armchairs in the suite and sat him down in it.

"I need a drink," Drake said. "Have one?"

"Why not?"

"Will you pour?"

"Sure."

Mundy poured two glasses of brandy from a crystal decanter and handed Drake one. The man sipped it gratefully.

"We can't trust Adams," he said, touching his nose gingerly.

"He'll probably get the job done."

"Yeah, for the wrong reasons," Drake said. "He doesn't care about the sword, or the politics."

"What do the reasons matter?" Mundy asked. "As long as the job gets done."

"That's not the way politics work."

"Well, the politics are your responsibility, not mine," Mundy said.

"I want that sword, Captain."

"We'll get it, Mr. Drake," the captain assured him. "I have my orders."

"Yes, you do."

"But the girl—"

"You let Adams worry about the girl," Drake said. "That's what he's here for."

"I should be going," Mundy said, putting his glass down.

"Before you do," Drake said, "my man should be along soon."

"I thought he'd be here today."

"He'll be here tonight," Drake said. "Make sure he meets Sheriff Potts, Mr. Connelly, and, I suppose, Adams."

"Do you want to see him tonight?"

"No," Drake said, touching his nose again. "I'm going to have another glass of brandy and go to sleep. I'll see him in the morning."

"Okay."

Mundy started for the door, then stopped.

"How will I know him?" he asked. "Some secret handshake or something?"

"Don't be a dunce," Drake said. "He's a tall Japanese, and his name is Ki. Believe me, you can't miss him."

TWELVE

Noah Bain watched the girl undress.

Her name was Betty. She was young, with small, firm breasts; pale, smooth skin; and lustrous black hair. He'd picked her out the moment he laid eyes on her.

Bain picked out small towns for him and his men to hole up in between jobs. They rarely stayed more than two or three months, though. After that they'd move on, pick another one.

This one was called Serenity.

He never chose a whore. He left that to Bledsoe and the other men. He usually picked a girl from town. It wasn't that hard to find one. They usually slept with him, thinking he'd take them away with him when he left. And he never did.

This one, he had to admit, might be different.

Bledsoe slapped the whore on her big ass, leaving a red handprint.

She didn't mind. He was also fucking her from behind at the same time.

She was a big, fleshy blonde named Jessie. Bledsoe was a big man, and he hated small, skinny girls. He usually picked out the biggest girl in the whorehouse and, in this case, it was Jessie.

He pounded into her, her big butt coming back to meet his thrusts. She'd found his rhythm the first time they were together, and had had no problem matching it since.

Whenever he and his partners came back to town, they came back with money. She and some of the other girls in the house took a lot of it—whatever didn't go for whiskey. She didn't like Bledsoe; he wasn't a nice man, but he was a good fuck and he paid for the privilege. And she had no illusions about leaving town with him. She never would have wanted to, anyway.

"Come on, baby," she said. "That's it. Harder!"

Betty Holcomb reclined naked on the bed, thrusting her breasts at Bain, who was watching, naked, from the other end of the room.

"Come on, baby," Betty said. "I'm waitin' for you."

Bain walked to the bed. He was a homely man, built short and wide. He had powerful legs and thighs, a thick waist and chest, and lots of hair on his body. He would not have been Betty's first choice, but he was probably only the latest in a string of men who had fucked her and promised to take her away with them and then left her behind. She kept trying, though, and less and less did the appearance of the man matter to her. Bain might even have been called ugly, but he had money and—who knew?—he might actually turn out to be the one who did take her away.

He climbed on the bed with her and spread her legs open. His penis was like the rest of him: thick, squat, powerful. He pressed the head of his penis to her pussy, rubbed it up and down until she was nice and slick, and then pushed it in. After that, it was just him pounding into her until he grunted, spurted, and rolled off of her. He always finished quick and—as far as she was concerned—that was just something in his favor. He was already snoring. At least she didn't have to put up with his rutting for more than a few minutes at a time. Her friend Jessie—poor girl—said that her man, Bledsoe, could keep it up all night.

THIRTEEN

Captain Mundy was standing out in front of the club having a cigar when a rider came down the street. It was almost dark, but he could see clearly that the man was Japanese.

He could see that the man had spotted him, directed his horse over. As he got closer, Mundy could see he was in his early thirties, sat tall in the saddle, wore a black Stetson, a black vest and a thin, black mustache that framed his mouth. The other thing he noticed was the absence of a gun—any kind of gun. No pistol, no rifle.

"Captain Mundy?" the man asked.

"That's right."

"I'm Ki. Mr. Drake is expecting me."

"We're all expecting you, Ki," Mundy said. "It's good to meet you. Step down, I'll have someone take care of your horse."

Ki inclined his head in something that was a combination nod and bow, and dismounted.

"Where is Mr. Drake?" the Japanese asked.

"Mr. Drake had to turn in early," Mundy said. "He'll see you in the morning. First light."

"Is that when the posse will go out again?" Ki asked.

"Yes."

"May I be allowed something to eat?" Ki asked.

"Of course," Mundy said. "I'll have them seat you inside."

"That would bring attention to me," Ki said. "I'd rather eat somewhere more . . . private."

"That can be arranged. There's a little steak house down the street. And I believe Mr. Drake has you in the Chandler Hotel."

"Thanks."

"The sheriff's gonna want to talk to you," Mundy said. "Also Clint Adams."

"The Gunsmith?" Ki's inscrutable eyes looked surprised. "He's here?"

"He's a friend of Mr. Connelly's."

"That's very good," Ki said. "It's good to know there's someone competent involved. Oh, no offense meant."

"None taken," Mundy said. "Let me show you that steak house. Then I'll have your horse taken care of and let the sheriff know where you are."

"Perhaps you could tell Mr. Adams, first?"

"Sure," Mundy said, "why not? He's in the same hotel you are, and it's not far from the steak house. I'll tell him where you are."

When the knock came at Clint's door, he wasn't surprised. Could have been Connelly, or Mundy, or Drake. But he took his gun to the door with him anyway, because there was always the chance somebody wanted to kill him.

He lowered the gun when he saw it was Mundy.

"Sorry to bother you, but Drake's man just got here."

"Is he with you?" Clint looked in the hall.

"He's across the street having a steak," Mundy said. "Thought you might want to talk to him."

"What about the sheriff?"

"Fella said he wanted to talk to you first. I mean, after I told him you were here."

"Who is he? Do you know him?"

"Never met him before, but he should be helpful in this matter."

"What makes you say that?"

"He's Japanese. Name's Ki."

Clint left his hotel room and walked across the street. The restaurant was two stores down from the little saloon where'd he'd talked with Eddie Castro.

He spotted Ki right away. It wasn't hard. The only Japanese in the place, the few other customers were seated across the room from him. They obviously found him interesting, because they were watching him eat. Clint was willing to bet they had never seen a Japanese man before. Clint had. In fact, Clint had heard of this Japanese man before. Marshal Custis Long had once told Clint about Jessie Starbuck and her partner/bodyguard, Ki. The marshal had worked with both of them before, and spoke very highly of them. Clint had never met either, but was about to.

As he approached the table, Ki took the reins.

"Mr. Adams?"

"That's right."

"Please, have a seat," Ki said, standing and shaking hands. "It's an honor to meet you. Deputy Marshal Long has spoken very highly of you."

Clint sat, accepted the slight, seated bow from Ki in lieu of a handshake.

"He's told me good things about you, too."

"Can I offer you something?"

A waiter came over at that moment, so Clint answered Ki and spoke to the waiter at the same time.

"I'll have some coffee. Thanks."

"I was very happy when Captain Mundy told me you were involved in this matter," Ki said while cutting off a piece of steak.

"And I was surprised to hear you were involved," Clint said,. "Are you alone? Without Jessie?"

"She didn't consider this to be her business," Ki said.

"And it is yours?"

"Someone made it mine."

"Mr. Drake?"

"Drake?" Ki frowned. "No, I was speaking of Akemi Tanaka."

"Drake didn't send you here?"

"No," Ki said. "Tanaka requested my involvement, and I couldn't refuse."

"Well, you should know that Drake is calling you 'his man,'" Clint said.

"Is that a fact?" Ki raised an eyebrow. "Then I'm afraid the man's a liar."

"On top of everything else that he is," Clint said.

"Am I to take it he is not going to be helpful?" Ki asked.

"Just the opposite, I'm afraid, "Clint said, "although you may not think so."

"Explain, please."

"Well, you're here to get the sword back," Clint said. "That's all Mr. Drake and Captain Mundy are concerned with."

"And you?"

"I want to bring back a murderer," Clint said, "and return Elizabeth Connelly to her father."

Ki frowned.

"I am afraid I didn't have all the facts," he said. "Could you fill me in, please?"

"Sure."

FOURTEEN

Clint was surprised to find that no one had informed Ki of what had happened to the Connelly women. He'd heard that some employees had been killed when the sword was stolen, but nothing about the man's family.

"I'm disappointed," Ki said when Clint was finished.

"With who?"

"Tanaka didn't inform me of all the facts," Ki said. "And neither did anyone connected with the U.S. government."

"I wonder why," Clint said. "Surely they knew you'd eventually find out."

"It would be unavoidable," Ki said.

"Are you still going to help?" Clint asked.

"Certainly," Ki said. "I'll do everything I can to bring the unfortunate girl back."

"Actually," Clint said, "she's a young woman, about twenty-two."

"All the more reason to rescue her," Ki said. "There's no telling what's being done to her."

"My thoughts exactly."

"These men, Noah Bain and Travis Bledsoe, I've never heard of them."

"Apparently, they've been confining their activities to Texas, so far."

"The Starbuck ranch is in South Texas," Ki said.

"So is Labyrinth," Clint said, "where I spend much of my leisure time, and I had never heard of them before. I suppose they've only been hitting West and North Texas. Maybe East Texas."

"We'll have to find out for sure," Ki said, "so that we know where to look."

"We can ask the sheriff."

"I haven't met him."

"We can go to his office as soon as you finish eating. That is, unless you want to rest—"

"I'm fine," Ki said. "And I'm finished. Let's go?"

"Sure."

Ki paid the bill and then they walked outside. The Japanese donned his black Stetson, and Clint noticed that he wore rope sandals, not boots, on his feet. He also noted the fact that Ki did not wear a gun, but he doubted the man was without a weapon—somewhere.

FIFTEEN

Clint walked Ki over to the sheriff's office and the two men entered. This time Clint could smell the coffee, and Potts was sitting behind his desk, drinking a cup. There was another man there, too, also wearing a badge.

"Mr. Adams," Potts said. "I thought we wouldn't be seein' you until mornin'."

"Something came up, Sheriff."

"Well, this is one of my deputies, Hal Sweet."

"Adams," the deputy said, nervously. "It's a pleasure."

Clint nodded at the man, who appeared to be in his early thirties.

"This is Ki," Clint said. "Ki, this is Sheriff Potts."

"Mr. Ki," Potts said, nodding. The deputy just stared.

"Just Ki," the Japanese said.

"Ki has been sent here to help find the Bain gang and rescue Elizabeth."

"Good," Potts said, "we can use all the help we can get."

"Oh," Clint added, "and he's going to help get the sword back to Japan."

"Ah," Potts said. "Wait, is this the man Mr. Drake has been waitin' for?"

"Apparently," Clint said, "but according to Ki, he's not Drake's man."

"I represent Mr. Tanaka," Ki said. "He's the one who requested my presence. It was certainly arranged through the United States government, but I'm not aware of any allegiance I should have to a man named Drake."

Potts couldn't help himself from grinning.

"That's gonna come as a surprise to Mr. Drake, I'll bet."

"Won't be his first surprise," Clint said.

Potts laughed.

"I am missing something?" Ki asked.

"Oh, Clint popped Drake in the nose earlier today," Potts said. "Pretty much broke it."

"You attacked him?" Ki asked.

"I couldn't stop myself."

"Won't this make it difficult for you and he to cooperate?"

"Believe me," Clint said. "It was impossible before that."

"Well, have a seat, gents. Hal, get our guests some coffee."

"None for me," Ki said.

"Me, neither. We just came from the steak house across from the hotel. I just wanted you and Ki to meet, since he'll be coming with us tomorrow."

"Good," Potts said, "we can use all the help we can get. The gang has a good head start on us."

"Sheriff, Ki and I had never heard of the Bain gang until we came here," Clint said. "And we both spend a lot of time in South Texas."

"As far as I know, their activities have been concentrated in West and North Texas," Potts said. "Maybe they'll expand—that is, if we don't catch 'em."

"Have they ever kidnapped anyone before this?" Ki asked.

"No. That's what's so odd."

"It's also odd to me that they'd take the sword," Clint said. "I mean, if they were looking for money and things of value."

"Anyone looking at that sword," Ki said, "would realize that it is valuable."

"You mean beyond its value to the Japanese government?" Clint asked.

"I mean, it is worth a lot of money."

"It's worth a lot of money if they can get somebody to buy it," Clint said.

"That's a good point," Potts said.

"If they're looking to sell Elizabeth and the sword," Clint said, "they're going to need two buyers."

"Not one?" Potts asked.

"People dealing in slave trade don't generally buy swords, and it pretty much works the other way around, too," Clint said.

"What if they took the girl just to . . . you know, use her?" Potts asked.

"Or sell her back to her father," the deputy chimed in.

"I think Connelly would have heard from them by now if that was the case, Deputy," Clint said. "No, I think they're going to be looking for two buyers."

"How does that help us?" Potts asked.

"Well, I know some people who know some people who might be able to come up with some buyers' names," Clint explained.

"And how do intend to put that to good use?" Potts asked.

"I'll have to send some telegrams tomorrow, before we leave."

"We're leavin' kinda early," Potts said. "The telegraph office won't be open."

"You're the law," Clint said. "You could open it. Wake up the key operator?"

"I could do that, I guess," Potts said.

"I'd be happy to wake him up," Deputy Sweet said with a smile. "Todd always thinks he's so special because he works the key."

Clint looked at Potts.

"Fine," the sheriff said, "Hal, get Todd up at first light. We'll send some telegrams before we ride out."

"Yesss!" Sweet said.

"Okay," Clint said. "Ki's been riding all day, so he needs to get some rest. So do I. We'll see you out front first thing."

"I'll have the key operator awake and ready," Sweet promised.

"And enjoy doin' it," Potts said.

"What about the rest of your posse?" Clint asked.

"I think I'm going to keep it the five of us," the sheriff said. "You, Ki, me, and my two deputies."

"Is that by choice," Clint said, "or are there slim pickings?"

"There are plenty of storekeepers who want to go back out—to get away from their wives, or their jobs, I think—but they might end up shootin' one of us. I'd say it's a little of both."

"We'll see you all in the morning, then," Clint said.

Ki inclined his head, and he and Clint left the sheriff's office.

"Not much of a posse," Clint said, outside.

"I have a feeling," Ki said, "that you and I would do just as well—or better—alone."

"That's what I was thinking, too, actually," Clint said. "We just need the sheriff to show us where he lost the trail."

"Then we can go from there," Ki said.

SIXTEEN

Elizabeth Connelly tried the door again, for the hundredth—or was it the thousandth?—time. She didn't know why she expected to suddenly find it unlocked, at some point. Maybe just wishful thinking that one of the gang might have a change of heart and unlock the door to let her escape.

Only she didn't want to escape. She just wanted to get out of that room and get her hands on a gun. Although her mother had been felled by a hail of bullets, she had decided—calling on everything she'd seen and heard since that day—that it was Travis Bledsoe who was responsible for her death. He was the one she wanted to kill the most. And then perhaps his boss, this Noah Bain they all talked about. She hadn't even met him, yet, but she wanted to kill him.

She wondered why none of the men had come in to rape her yet. Wasn't that what men like this did? Rape their female captives? Or were they not touching her because they wanted to sell her back to her father? Or to someone else?

She had a cot in the room, and a small wooden table. She'd been brought some meals, which had been set on that table. She'd held out as long as she could, but she'd actually eaten the last couple. After all, if she was going to kill somebody, she needed to keep up her strength.

At the moment, there was a tin plate and a wooden spoon on the table, from her last meal. They'd been careful not to bring her any knives or forks. Maybe they thought she'd kill herself with them. They certainly didn't act fearful that she'd kill any of them.

There was a window, but it was small and up high. The building was adobe, and while there was no glass in the window it was too small—and too inaccessible— for her to use as an escape route.

There were no other sounds in the building. She didn't know how many other rooms there were because she had been blindfolded when they brought her in, but they didn't seem to have any other captives.

She stood up, walked to the door, and tried the door knob again.

Still locked.

SEVENTEEN

Clint woke the next morning, knowing there was a lot to do before he ever got on a horse. He dressed quickly and went down to the lobby. When he got there, he found Ki and Don Connelly waiting.

"I just met Ki," Connelly said. "We got the club to make some breakfast for you before you leave."

"That's good," Clint said. "Will Drake be there?"

"Probably," Connelly said.

"Is he planning on having me arrested for punching him?" Clint asked.

"No," Connelly said, "I don't think so. That would hold up the posse, wouldn't it?"

"You think he cares?"

"If he cares at all for the sword," Ki said, "then he cares."

"Come on," Connelly said, "let's get some breakfast."

At the club, they found the rest of the posse—the three lawmen—along with Captain Mundy and Drake. The government man's eyes were black and blue. A breakfast had been laid out on the table so that the men could help themselves. There were eggs, bacon, potatoes, and biscuits, along with pots of coffee.

The look Drake gave Clint was blood murder, helped along by the fact that his eyes were bloodshot. Clint was surprised. He didn't think he'd hit the man that hard. He almost felt bad enough to apologize.

Mundy did the honors, introducing Ki to Drake. The two men quickly went to a corner for a conversation.

"What's that about?" Mundy asked.

"I think Ki's telling Drake to stop referring to him as his man," Clint said, "because he's not."

"Then who sent him?" Mundy asked.

"You better take that up with Drake," Clint said. "I'm going to get some breakfast."

Clint went over and stood next to Hal Sweet, who was filling his plate.

"You get the key operator up?" he asked.

"Oh yeah," Sweet said. "He'll be over there when we get there."

"Good."

All the men attacked the breakfast buffet, Drake looking even unhappier now that Ki had clearly laid down the law.

When Clint finished eating, he grabbed Sweet and told the sheriff they would go over and send the telegrams, and then meet in front of his office.

"Okay," Potts said, "let's make it half an hour, but no later."

"Right," Clint said.

Sweet took Clint over to the telegraph office, where the sleepy, unhappy key operator was, indeed, waiting. Clint had already written down his telegrams in his room, one to Rick Hartman in Labyrinth, and one to Talbot Roper in Denver. Both men had their ear to the ground and contacts all over the country. If there was any word of a samurai sword being up for sale, they'd hear it.

Telegrams sent, Clint and Sweet went to saddle their horses.

The posse members met in front of the sheriff's office. When Clint and Sweet rode up, the others were all there. Mundy was there, too, but probably just to see them off. Drake was nowhere in sight.

"You and Drake get into it?" Clint asked Ki.

"Not exactly," Ki said, "but I can see why you popped him in the nose. I almost did it myself. But I think he got the message."

Clint turned to Potts.

"We've got no supplies, Adams, except what we each normally carry," Potts explained. "I wanted to make sure we traveled light."

"I don't have a problem making a cold camp, Sheriff," Clint said.

"We've got some coffee and beef jerky, but that's it."

"Fine."

"You mind if I take the lead?" Potts asked.

"Sheriff," Clint said, "this is your posse. I expect you to take the lead."

At least, Clint thought, until they reached that point where Potts lost the gang's trail.

They were about to ride off when they heard another horse approaching. Clint turned and saw Don Connelly riding toward them.

"I didn't know he was comin'," Sweet said.

"Who is it?" Ki asked.

"The girl's father," the second deputy, Johnny King, said.

When Connelly reached them both, Clint and the sheriff turned to face him.

"No, Donny," Clint said.

"She's my daughter, Clint," Connelly said. "I have a right to go."

"That may be so, sir," Sheriff Potts said, "but it's not a good idea."

"Why not?"

Potts looked to Clint for help.

"Donny, if the kidnappers try to contact you to sell her back, you'll have to be here. Who knows what they'll do if you're not?"

Connelly stared at Clint, then rubbed his hand over his eyes. He wanted to argue, but he didn't have the energy.

"Oh, all right," he said. "I guess you're right."

"Go back to the Cattleman's Club and get some more rest," Clint said. "We'll be back as soon as we can—with Elizabeth."

Clint turned to Potts.

"Ready to go, Sheriff."

EIGHTEEN

After they had ridden about an hour and it was full daylight, Clint asked, "Do we go by the ranch?"

"Right by it," Potts said. "We tracked them from there."

"Can we stop?"

"What for?"

"I just want to have a look," Clint said. "In fact, I'll stop and you can keep going."

"That won't do any good," Potts said. "I'm supposed to show you where we lost the trail."

"How far is it?"

"A day's ride."

"I won't take long," Clint said, "and I'll be able to catch up to you."

"Oh, all right," Potts said. "If that's what you want."

When they were within sight of the ranch, Potts said, "There," pointing.

"Is there anybody there now?" Clint asked.

"Not that I know of," Potts said. "I think Castro is still in town."

"Okay," Clint said. "You go ahead, I'll catch up."

"I'll ride along with you," Ki said to Clint. "I'd like to see the scene, too."

"I don't mind," Clint said.

"All right," Potts said. "Maybe the three of us should come with you, too."

"No, keep going," Clint said. "Maybe going over old ground you'll see something you missed the first time."

The sheriff gave up.

"Let's go, boys."

The three lawmen rode off; Clint and Ki rode to the ranch house.

Clint and Ki dismounted in front of the house, secured their horses, and went up the stairs. They saw blood on the floor in the doorway, and stepped over it. There were a few bullet holes in the front door.

The inside of the house was in shambles. Castro had said the men rode their horses into the house.

They found blood on the floor inside the house, probably the cook's. The crippled ranch hand's blood would already have soaked into the ground outside, or blown away.

"Split up?" Ki asked.

"Why not?" Clint said. "I'll take the upstairs."

Clint didn't know what he expected to see, but if you were going to do a job right you had to start at the beginning. This was where everything began.

All the bedrooms had been ransacked. Things the men had obviously found worthless were broken and scattered on the floor. Anything of value had been removed. Clint wondered if they had ridden their horses up the stairs.

He went back downstairs but didn't see Ki anywhere until the man called out, "Clint?"

"Where are you?"

"Down the hall."

Clint located the voice and saw Ki standing at the end of the hallway.

"In here," Ki said, and then disappeared into a room.

Clint walked down the hall and found the room. Ki was standing in front of two empty pegs on the wall.

"This must be where the sword was," Ki said.

Clint looked around.

"There are no other swords," Clint said.

"Did you think there would be?" Ki asked.

"I don't know. Connelly said he was interested in swords. I thought he'd have more."

"That one had to cost a fortune," Ki said. "It's a collection all by itself."

Clint looked around the room, which had obviously been Connelly's office. There was nothing else of value in it. Oddly, though, it had not been ransacked, like the rest of the house.

"They were after the sword," Clint said.

"What?" Ki asked.

"They were specifically after the sword."

"How could they have known about it?" Ki asked.

"I don't know, but look at the room. Whoever took the sword walked in here, grabbed it, and walked out."

Clint walked to the desk and opened three drawers before he found what he was looking for: a cashbox. He took it out and opened it.

"See? There's still money in here." He returned the box to the drawer.

"So they were hired to come here and steal the sword," Ki said. "And were probably told to make it look like a robbery."

"Elizabeth was here, so they decided to grab her, too."

"We still don't know why."

"I haven't seen her since she was a little girl," Clint said, "but I was told she's beautiful."

"So they took her to sell or keep," Ki said, "for a while, anyway."

"Someone suggested that maybe one of the men took a fancy to her," Clint said.

"Maybe," Ki said, "but how long will his partners let him have her until they want some, too?" Ki asked.

"I know."

"Seen enough?" KI asked.

"Yes," Clint said. "At least now we know we're dealing with men who were probably hired for the job."

"Now all we have to do is find out by who," Ki said.

NINETEEN

Clint and Ki left the ranch house and rode back to where they'd split from the others. From that point, they began to follow the trail left by the three lawmen.

"I think we have a tail," Clint said.

"I know. Whoever it is followed us from town."

"So why didn't he continue to follow Potts and his men?" Clint wondered.

"Maybe they think we have a better chance of finding the gang than the lawmen do."

"Why don't we ask him?"

"Okay."

The rider reined in, looked around anxiously, then looked at the ground. He was still looking when Ki dropped down on him from a tree limb, taking him off his horse cleanly. Ki immediately got to his feet and looked down at the man. Clint came out from behind a bush.

"On your feet," he said.

The man staggered to his feet, glared at Ki and Clint.

"Castro?" Clint asked.

"You know him?"

"Yes," Clint said, "Eddie Castro. He works for Don Connelly. In fact, he was the only surviving witness."

"What's he doing following us?" Ki asked.

"I don't know," Clint said, then looked at the boy. "What are you doing following us, Eddie?"

"I have to get Elizabeth back," he said. "It's my fault they took her."

"How do you figure that?" Ki asked.

"I should have done somethin'," the kid said. "If I had, maybe they wouldn't have took her."

"I told you, kid," Clint said. "You would've been dead, too."

"Yeah, but maybe they wouldn't have took her."

Clint looked at Ki, who shrugged.

"Wait a minute," Clint said. "There's something else going on here, isn't there, Eddie?"

"W-what do you mean?" Castro suddenly looked like a cornered rat.

"There's another reason you're out here, isn't there?" Clint asked.

"I don't know what ya mean," Castro said.

"Yeah, you do, kid," Clint said. "Were you and Elizabeth seeing each other?"

"What? No." Castro stuck his hands deep into his pockets. "She don't even know I'm alive."

"But you'd like her to know, wouldn't you?" Clint asked.

"Well . . . yeah, who wouldn't?"

"So you think if you save her, she'll notice you?" Ki asked.

Castro shrugged and said, "Maybe."

"Do you even have a gun?" Clint asked.

"Sure."

"Let's see it," Clint said. "Where is it?"

"In my saddlebags."

"Get it."

Castro went to his horse, which had only wandered a few feet, and took his gun out of a saddlebag.

"Let me have it."

Castro handed it to Clint. It was an old Navy Colt, big and heavy and ill-cared for.

"This thing will blow up in your hand the first time you fire it," Clint said, handing the gun to Ki. "You got a rifle?"

"N-no."

"Okay, kid," Clint said. "Turn around and head home. The only thing you'd accomplish out here is to get yourself, or one of us, killed."

"B-but I can help."

"You can't help," Clint said. "You're useless."

"I can—I can take care of the horses."

"Not my horse," Clint said. "He'd bite your fingers off."

"No he wouldn't," Castro insisted. "I'm good with horses."

"Well, you'd have to offer a lot more than that," Clint said. "Go on home."

"Gimme my gun," the kid said.

"No," Clint said. "You'll blow your hand off, or shoot yourself in the foot. Just go home!"

Castro looked angry first, and then looked as if he was going to cry.

Clint went and got Castro's horse and walked it over.

"Get on."

Castro struggled to get into the saddle. Jesus, Clint thought, he can't even ride.

Clint turned the horse, said, "Now get!" and slapped it

on the rump. The horse took off running, with Eddie Castro bouncing around in the saddle.

"What do we do with this?" Ki asked, holding Castro's gun.

"Toss it," Clint said. "It's no good."

"What if he comes back and finds it?"

"You're right," Clint said. "Let's take it with us and toss it off a cliff or something."

Ki nodded, stuck the gun in his saddlebag. The men mounted up.

"Let's catch up with the others," Clint said.

TWENTY

"Okay," Noah Bain said to Bledsoe, "tell me again why you took the girl."

"You ain't seen her yet, Noah," Bledsoe said. "Or you wouldn't have to ask me that."

"But I am askin'," Bain said. "You just made our job harder, Travis."

"Naw," Bledsoe said, "just take a look at her, Noah. That's all I'm askin'. We got lots of options with this girl. Lots of 'em."

"Like a posse comin' after us for kidnappin'?" Bain asked.

"If there's a posse there's a posse," Bledsoe said. "If they're comin' after us for murder, what difference does kidnappin' make?"

Bain poked Bledsoe in the chest.

"I told you not to make a mess, didn't I?" Bain said.

"What was I supposed to do?" Bledsoe said. "The bitch came to the door shootin'. You weren't there, Noah."

"No, I wasn't," Bain said. "Maybe next time I should be."

"Yeah, fine," Bledsoe said, "but take a look at the girl before you make any decisions."

"Yeah, yeah, okay," Bain said. "I'll take a look, just to see what all the fuss is about."

Elizabeth heard the lock open on her door, sat on the cot with her knees drawn up to her chest. The door opened and a squat, ugly man who radiated power—physical strength—walked in. He stopped short and stared at her.

"Good God," he said. "Stand up . . . now!"

She stood, kept her hands at her side.

"Jesus," he said.

"Are you the boss?" she asked. "This man Bain I heard them talking about?"

"I'm Bain," he said, "and if you point out the man who told you my name I'll cut out his tongue."

She shivered, because she knew he meant it.

"My people tell me you didn't fight when they took you. Why would that be?"

"Honestly?"

"Yeah, honestly."

"I was hoping to have a chance to kill your man—the big one."

"Bledsoe?" he asked. "Travis?"

"If that's his name."

"Why Travis?"

"I blame him," she said. "He was in charge."

"He reports to me," Bain said. "Does that make me responsible, too?"

"Yes, it does."

"So you want to kill me, too?" Bain asked.

"Yes."

"Have you ever killed anyone before?"

"No."

"But you think you can do it?"

"Kill you and your man Bledsoe?" she asked. "Oh, yes, I could do it."

"You know, I believe you." Bain said. "Bledsoe said you were special."

"He did?"

"Yeah, he did," Bain said, "but he don't even know how special."

"If I'm so special," she said, "let me go."

Bain laughed.

"And if I let you go, would you run home?" he asked.

"Of course," she said, then added, "as soon as I kill you and Bledsoe."

Bain shook his head.

"I don't know what I'm gonna do with you, girl, but one thing I do know."

"What's that?"

"I sure as hell ain't lettin' you go!"

He backed out of the room and closed the door, then stood there for a minute. Never before had a woman taken Noah Bain's breath away. His first reaction had been visceral and primal—he'd wanted to cross the room, tear off her clothes, and rape her. She was so damn fresh, clean, and breathtakingly beautiful that he'd wanted nothing more than to defile her.

And yet he hadn't.

He'd told her the truth. He didn't know what to do with her. But until he made up his mind, he was going to see to it that nobody touched her.

TWENTY-ONE

"She wants to do what?" Bledsoe asked.

"Kill you," Bain said.

"That little bitch!" he said incredulously. "I'll tear her up!"

"You won't touch her."

"What?"

"You heard me," Bain said.

They were in the house Bain was using as his headquarters. Actually, it was Betty's house.

"What are you talkin' about?"

"You said she was special," Bain said. "You told me to have a look at her, and I did. And I agree: She's very special."

"You want her for yourself, don't you?" Bledsoe demanded.

"I haven't decided what to do with her, but I know one thing."

"What?"

"I don't want anyone to touch her. You got that, Travis?"

"I got it," Bledsoe said. "You think I wanna damage the property? You know what we can get for her in Mexico? Or somewhere like—"

"Like what?" Bain asked.

"You know, one of those foreign countries."

"Yeah, I do know," Bain said.

Bledsoe looked around for Betty. The girl claimed she wasn't a whore, but she did everything a whore did. And she was friends with Jessie, who definitely was a whore.

"Where's your girl?" Bledsoe asked. "What does she think about you wanting the Connelly girl for yourself?"

"Time for you to get out, Travis," Bain said. "While you can."

"I'm goin'."

"Make damn sure the rest of the men know not to touch that girl."

"I'll tell 'em."

He ran in to Betty as he was leaving.

"Count the days," he said. "They're numbered."

"What did he mean by that?"

"He's an idiot," Bain said. "Get undressed."

"Eager, aren't you?"

Bain's penis had been hard since he first saw Elizabeth.

"You have no idea."

TWENTY-TWO

When Clint and Ki caught up to the three lawmen, they were crouched on their heels, examining the ground. They looked up as the two men rode up on them.

"Looking for a good place to make a campfire?" Ki asked.

"Too early," Clint said. "There's still daylight."

Potts stood up.

"I thought I saw somethin'," he said. "Mount up!" he said to his deputies.

Clint and Ki exchanged a glance as the deputies and the sheriff got on their horses.

"What's going on, Sheriff?" Clint asked.

"Ride on ahead," Potts said to his deputies.

Sweet said, "Yes, sir," and looked embarrassed about something.

"You didn't see something on the ground that you missed days ago, Sheriff, did you?" Ki said.

"No," Potts said. "Johnny wants to go back."

"Why?" Clint asked.

"He's young and afraid," Potts said.

"Afraid of who?"

"Bledsoe."

"Not Bain?" Clint asked.

"No, it's not Bain who kills; it's Bledsoe."

"And your deputy knows Bledsoe?"

"He knows of him," Potts said. "Everybody in West Texas knows Bledsoe."

"Was Bledsoe well known before he joined up with Bain?" Clint asked.

"Let's say he was known."

"And Bain?"

"He was known, too," Potts said.

"Posters on either of them?"

Potts thought a moment, then said, "Yeah, there were."

"For murder?"

"Not that I can remember."

"How long have they been together?"

"A few years."

"And since they got together they're both wanted for murder?"

"No," Potts said. "Bledsoe is."

"So Bledsoe does all the killing?"

"That's the way it seems."

"And your deputy knows that."

"Yeah."

Clint looked at Ki, who shrugged an "I-don't-care" shrug.

"Let him go home, Sheriff."

"Why?"

"We don't need him if he's scared," Clint said, "and if he knows Bledsoe, he shouldn't be here, anyway."

"Maybe he's scared of him," Ki said, "but he could also admire him."

"All the more reason we don't need him," Clint said.

"Well . . . okay."

"And how about Sweet?"

"Sweet?" Potts said, smiling. "He admires you. You want to send him home for that?"

"Not unless it gets in the way of him doing his job," Ki said.

"It won't," Potts said.

TWENTY-THREE

It was almost dusk when Sheriff Potts said, "This is the place."

Johnny King had headed back to town three hours earlier. His dispatch had confused Sweet, but the young deputy hadn't said a word.

They all reined in and dismounted.

"The trail died here," Potts said. "You can see how hard the ground is, here, and there's no brush, no foliage."

"Bain is smart," Clint said.

"You think Bain rode them over this ground on purpose?" Ki asked.

"He's the leader, right?" Clint asked. "Bledsoe is the killer, Bain is the leader."

They both started to walk the ground. Clint had no idea how good a tracker Ki was. He was fair. If Ki was better, let him show it and Clint would follow him.

"What now?" Potts asked. "It's gettin' dark."

"Have Sweet build a fire, put on some coffee," Clint said. "We'll camp here."

"Okay."

Potts turned, but Clint called out to him.

"Sheriff?"

"Yeah?"

"How far are you willing to go?"

Potts stopped to think.

"Well, I'm pursuing a murderer," he said. "Jurisdiction don't figure in too much."

"Okay, so all the way?"

"All the way, Adams."

"Tell me: You think Mundy's out here somewhere with a troop of men?"

"I don't see how he cannot be, to tell you the truth," Potts said. "The government really wants that sword."

"But the sword belongs to Connelly, right?" Clint said. "I mean, they can't really take it from him."

"Who knows?" Potts said. "They're the government, right?"

Potts went to tell Sweet to make a fire. Clint turned, saw Ki walking the ground with his head down. He decided to try the opposite direction.

Before either man could pick up the trail the sheriff had lost, it got dark. They'd have to wait until morning to continue.

Clint and Ki returned to camp in time for Sweet to hand them each a cup of coffee.

"Nothin'?" Potts asked.

"Not yet," Clint said.

"If there's a trail to find, one of us will find it," Ki said, confidently.

"You sound real sure of yourself," Sweet said.

Ki looked at the young deputy.

"We'll find it because we won't stop until we do," Ki explained. "It's that simple."

"But what if there is no trail to find?" young Sweet asked.

"That can't be," Clint said.

"Why not?"

"Because we're not dealing with ghosts," Ki said. "If they came this way, they left a trail."

"And you can follow it, even after a few days?" Sweet asked.

"We saw the tracks at the house," Ki said. "We can match them up."

Clint had a bad thought. If, as Sweet suggested, there was no trail here to find, that would mean only one thing—that the sheriff had led them on a wild-goose chase. And he would have only done that if he was working with the Bain gang.

Clint saw Ki watching him. Was the Japanese thinking the same thing?

"We better set a watch," Clint said, squatting by the fire. "Just in case."

"Just in case what?" Sweet asked.

"Just in case we need to," Ki said. He looked at Clint. "I'll go first."

"I'll relieve you," Clint said. That way he and Ki would be able to talk while the two lawmen were asleep.

TWENTY-FOUR

When Clint came to the fire to relieve Ki, the Japanese handed him a cup of coffee and asked, "Are you thinking what I'm thinking?"

"If there's no trail I am," Clint said, keeping his voice low. He squatted across the fire from Ki.

"That stuff about Deputy King wanting to go back," Ki said. "What if Potts wanted him to go back?"

"To do what?"

Ki shrugged.

"Send somebody a telegram?"

"If that was the case, why wouldn't he have just left him behind?"

"That's another thing I was thinking."

"What's that?"

"Potts left town and took both deputies with him," Ki said. "Who's minding the store back there?"

"Good thought. The army?"

"What's the army care what happens in Chandlerville?" Ki asked. "They're only concerned about the sword."

"You're a suspicious guy, aren't you?"

"Hey," Ki said, "you've been having the same thoughts, right?"

"Only since we got here," Clint said. "And only if we don't find a trail tomorrow."

"I guess I better turn in then," Ki said.

"I thought you Japanese warriors didn't need much sleep?"

Ki stood up.

"You got me mixed up with somebody else, white man," he said.

Clint laughed.

"Who's relieving you?" Ki asked.

"Sweet."

"He seems okay to me," Ki said. "A little young and naïve, but okay."

"Those are the ones you really have to watch out for," Clint said.

"And you call me suspicious."

Sweet was yawning when he got to the fire to relieve Clint.

"Mornin'," Clint said. "I hope you can stay awake."

"Don't worry about me," Sweet said, rubbing his eyes, "I'm as alert as a cat."

"Here, take this," Clint said, handing him a cup of coffee, "it'll help keep you that way."

"Thanks." Sweet squatted by the fire to drink his coffee.

"I'll see you later."

As Clint turned to walk away, Sweet said, "Mr. Adams?"

"It's Clint, Deputy Sweet," Clint said. "Just call me Clint."

"Okay, Clint, uh, can I ask you something before you turn in?"

"Sure, go ahead."

"You plan on bringing Bain and Bledsoe and the rest back alive?"

"Does it matter to you?" Clint asked.

"Yes, sir," Sweet said, "actually, it does."

"Well, I'll tell you what," Clint said. "I plan to bring Elizabeth Connelly back alive. As far as the others are concerned, it's going to be up to them. That answer your question?"

"Yes, sir," Sweet said, but he didn't sound all that sure.

TWENTY-FIVE

Sweet woke the others at first light, with coffee for all. They'd had jerky for dinner, and then more jerky for breakfast. Clint and Ki got to work, walking the ground, looking for any sign that someone had passed this way. If they didn't find any, then they were going to have to question the sheriff—something Clint wasn't looking forward to. He didn't like to think of lawmen gone bad, but he'd run into enough of them to know they were always out there.

"I got 'em!" Ki shouted.

Clint, Potts, and Sweet ran over to where he was standing.

"You sure it's them?" Potts asked.

"Somebody was here in the past few days," Ki said.

Clint looked down at the ground. Whatever Ki had seen, he wasn't seeing it.

"Here," Ki said, pointing, "and here. "See? Faint outlines of hoof prints, and over on the stone. Scuff marks."

"Wow," Sweet said. "I never would have found that."

"The tracks point this way," Ki said, pointing north.

"Any idea how many?" Potts asked.

"We'll have to keep following them to see that," Ki said.

"Then let's get started," Clint said.

"Mount up!" Potts said.

Within a mile, the tracks were visible enough for all in the group to easily spot.

"Damn," Potts said.

"What?" Clint asked.

"All I had to do was keep going north and I would've found them."

Clint didn't want to say it, but he'd been thinking that very same thing. Why had Potts turned back so quickly?

"How many are there?" Sweet asked. "I see . . . a lot."

"I see . . . about eight different horses," Ki said.

"Castro said they took the girl away on one of their horses," Potts said. "Probably Bledsoe's."

"So," Clint said, "Bain, Bledsoe, and six others."

"We need more men," Sweet said, looking at the others for confirmation.

"Not really," Ki said. "We've got the element of surprise on our side."

"You don't think they know there's a posse after them?" Pott asked.

"Oh, they know," Ki said, "but they think they lost you."

Potts face assumed a sour look as he said, "And they did. We only found them again thanks to you."

"Doesn't matter who found them," Clint said. "All that matters is that we did."

"*If* it's them," Sweet said.

"Come here," Ki said to Sweet, dismounting. The kid followed him.

"See that shoe? That's how we know it's them. I saw the same track back at the ranch house."

"I see it," Sweet said.

"Some tracks are the same," Ki told him, "and some aren't. You just have to look."

"Yes, sir."

"Let's keep movin'," Potts said. "I want to make good use of this day, now that we've found them."

Another mile and Ki held his hand up.

"What is it now?" Potts asked, sounding annoyed. He was apparently taking it hard that he could have picked the trail up again and didn't.

"They split up here," Ki said. "Four that way, four that way." He pointed east and west.

"Why?" Sweet asked.

"To throw us off," Clint said. "Split us up, too."

"So what do we do?" the deputy asked.

"Easy," Ki said. "Clint and I will go west, you and the sheriff can go east."

"Why do we go west?" Sweet asked when the Sheriff didn't argue.

"Takes you back toward your jurisdiction," Ki said.

"They're doubling back?" Sweet asked. "Why?"

"Just to throw us off, maybe," Clint said. "We'll only find out by following."

"Shouldn't one of us stay with one of you?" Sweet asked. "I mean, we got the badges."

"Come on, kid," Potts said. "It don't matter. If they want to do it that way, fine." Potts looked at Clint and Ki. "You find any of 'em, you bring 'em back to town, you hear? Alive."

"Sure, Sheriff," Clint said. "Alive."

"That's the plan," Ki said.

"Come on, Sweet," Potts said.

They wheeled their horses around and rode east.

"Okay," Clint said to Ki, "why are we going west?"

Ki got down from his horse and went down to one knee.

"See this track? It's deep. Real deep."

"Two people riding double?" Clint asked.

"That's what I'm thinking," Ki said. "Bledsoe and the girl, and I think where they're going, Bain's going, too."

"And the sword?"

"And the sword."

"Okay," Clint said, as Ki remounted. "West it is."

TWENTY-SIX

Clint and Ki came to a small town called Hardesty. The tracks they were following led right through it, but did show that they had stopped there. What they couldn't tell from the tracks was how long the riders had stopped. Hopefully someone in town would be able to tell them that.

They reined their horses in in front of the town's only saloon. Somebody inside had to have seen someone the size of Travis Bledsoe. Or somebody as beautiful as Elizabeth supposedly was.

"I'll do the talking," Clint said as they approached the saloon on foot.

"Why's that?"

"Small town," Clint said. "They probably haven't seen many Japanese here. We should hold you back in case we have to use that later."

"So you want me to be silent?"

"Completely."

Ki shrugged. He'd played the inscrutable Asian many times before.

They entered the saloon, attracted the attention of the half-dozen men there, because they were strangers, and also because Ki was strange looking.

They walked to the bar, where a mouth-breathing bartender stared at them.

"What's he?"

"What?" Clint asked.

"I said what the hell is he?" the man asked, looking at Ki.

"He's my servant," Clint said.

"Your what?"

"Servant," Clint said. "I pay him."

"For what?"

"To serve me."

"Does he talk?"

"No."

"He's funny-lookin'."

"He's foreign."

"Oh."

"Two beers, please."

"He drinks beer?"

"He does."

"Comin' up."

When the bartender brought the beers, Ki picked up Clint's and handed it to him, then picked up the other one and sipped it.

"He Chinese?" the bartender asked.

"No," Clint said, "Japanese."

"I ain't never seen no Japanese. Fact is, I ain't never heard of no Japanese. He sure do look Chinese, though."

"Don't keep saying that," Clint warned.

"Why not?"

"He don't like it."

"What'll he do?"

Clint shrugged. "There's no telling."

"Hmm." The bartender stared at Ki like he belonged in a cage.

"Hey!" Clint said.

"Huh?"

"Don't stare, either," Clint said. "He doesn't like it."

"What does he like?" the bartender asked.

"Beer," Clint said. "And answers."

"What kinda answers?"

"Some men came through town a few days ago," Clint said. "One was a big fella riding double with a girl—a pretty girl."

"So?"

"Did they stop here?"

The bartender studied Clint and Ki, then asked, "You law?"

"Yeah," Clint said, with a smirk, "he's a federal marshal."

The other men in the place, listening to the conversation, all snickered.

"We're tracking them," Clint said.

"Bounty hunters?"

"What else?" Clint asked with a shrug.

"Yeah," the bartender said, "yeah, they came through here."

"Did they stay overnight?"

"Nope," the man said. "They stopped just long enough."

"Long enough for what?"

"Long enough to pay us to stop anybody who was followin' them."

The other men all stood up from their tables and went for their guns.

TWENTY-SEVEN

Clint drew quickly and fired twice. Two men went down before they could clear their weapons.

Ki, moving at least as quickly, threw two knives, and two more men went down—only he hadn't thrown knives; they were metal stars with sharp edges.

The bartender and the remaining man froze where they were.

Clint pointed his gun at the bartender.

"I hope you got paid enough," he said.

"Not nearly."

"Where'd they go?"

"Just kept headin' west, as far as I know."

"Did they pay you in advance?"

"Yeah."

"Why would you go through with this if they paid you already?"

"They said they'd come back and kill us if we didn't," the bartender said.

"Well, now four of you are dead," Clint said, "and I can arrange for you to follow."

"No. Please."

Clint looked at Ki, who was checking bodies and disarming the remaining man. He'd also reclaimed the throwing stars and put them in his vest pockets.

"Dead?" Clint asked.

"Yes," Ki said.

"You said he was mute," the bartender said accusingly.

"I lied. You got a gun under the bar?"

"Yeah."

"Give it to me, by the barrel."

The bartender brought out a sawed-off shotgun, holding it by the barrel, and handed it over. Clint cracked it and let the shells drop out, then threw the shotgun out the door.

"When were they here?"

"Like you said, about three days ago."

"How long did they stay?"

"A few hours, long enough to eat."

"How did the girl look?"

"Fine," the man said. "She wasn't even fightin' them. It was like she wasn't no prisoner, at all."

That couldn't be right.

"Anybody else in town?" Clint asked.

"No," the bartender said. "It's just us. This is pretty much a ghost town. Population six."

"Now two," Clint said.

"Yeah," the bartender said, looking around, "now two."

Clint looked at Ki. "Feel like wiping out a whole town?" he asked.

"Let's just go and leave them," Ki said. "We got what we wanted."

Clint looked at the bartender. "You're a lucky man."

"Not so's you'd notice," the man said.

"You got any food?" Clint asked.

"Got some canned goods."

"Get them."

The man went behind the bar through a door that apparently led to what had once been a kitchen. He came out with a gunnysack that hung heavy with cans.

"I didn't give ya all I got," he said, handing it over.

"I wouldn't take all your food," Clint said, accepting the sack. "Come on, Ki."

They backed out of the saloon and mounted up. Clint watched their backs until they rode out of town.

TWENTY-EIGHT

"What were those things you used today?" Clint asked. "I've never seen anything like that."

They were camped for the night, miles from the town of Hardesty. They had coffee and jerky—the last of their jerky, so they didn't eat it. Instead, Clint dug into the cans the bartender had given him: beef stew and some peaches. They each took a can of beef stew.

Ki put his hand in his pocket and took one of the throwing stars out. He handed it to Clint.

"They're called *Shuriken*," he said. "Japanese throwing stars. Careful, they're sharp."

"I can see that," Clint said. He'd already cut one finger. "How do you throw them?"

"It takes training, and a lot of practice. I also have these," he said. He rolled up his sleeves to show Clint the throwing knives strapped to his arms.

"Impressive," Clint said. "And here I was thinking you didn't have any weapons."

He handed Ki back his *Shuriken*.

"You were fast," Ki said, "faster than I've ever seen."

Clint didn't comment, sipped his coffee.

"Does that come naturally?" Ki asked.

"Somewhat," Clint said. "I found at an early age that I had a natural affinity for guns. I could hit what I pointed at. And I was fast. But there was still plenty of practice in there, as well."

"But not anymore?"

"No, not anymore, "Clint said. "No more practice. I don't draw my gun unless I'm going to use it."

"You don't target shoot, or show off?" Ki asked.

"Not what I do," Clint said.

"That's admirable," Ki said. "Every other man I've ever known who is an expert marksman always has to prove it."

"When somebody dies, that's proof enough to me," Clint said

"I'll take first watch," Ki said.

"That's fine," Clint said. "Wake me in three."

"Or four," Ki said. "I'm not really tired."

"That from some Japanese training, too?" Clint asked.

"No," Ki said, "for some reason tonight I'm just not that tired."

Elizabeth couldn't sleep.

She kept expecting Noah Bain to come bursting through the door to rape her. His naked need had been very evident to her, and she didn't know how long he was going to be able to deny it—or why he was denying it.

Or worse, it could have been Bledsoe. With him she'd never know if he wanted to rape her, kill her . . . or both.

She wasn't worried about the rest of the gang, just those two. They seemed to be the leaders. But she didn't yet know which of them was the most dominant.

Bain seemed smarter than Bledsoe, but the bigger man seemed the most dangerous.

But staying awake was hard, tiring work, and in the end she did drift off to sleep.

TWENTY-NINE

Clint woke Ki with the toe of his boot, handed him a cup of coffee.

"What's Jessie Starbuck think of you taking this on?" Clint asked. "I mean, you're supposed to be her bodyguard, right?"

"When we ended the cartel, our relationship changed slightly. We are more like . . . partners, now."

"So why didn't she come with you?"

"Because I told her not to," Ki said. "This was not her affair. Besides, she has a business to run."

They finished their coffee, killed the fire, and packed up to ride.

"My guess is we'll find them today," Ki said as they mounted up.

"Your guess?"

"Or we'll lose them," he added.

"Why would we find them today?" Clint asked.

"They'll want to go to ground and wait," Ki said. "Not keep running. They'll figure that, sooner or later, the posse will give up and go back."

"And where do you figure they'll go to ground?"

"A hideout," Ki said. "A canyon, a cave, or maybe a small speck of a town."

"We just came through a small speck of a town," Clint said.

"Well, not a ghost town," Ki, said, "but one that will sustain them."

"Then they'll probably all be there," Clint said, "because my guess is they split up only to confound a posse. They'll come back together wherever they're hiding."

"So if the sheriff stays on their trail, we should meet up with him and Sweet, too," Ki said.

"Hopefully," Clint said. "We'll be able to use the extra firepower."

"Like I said," Ki added, "that's if we don't lose them again."

"Well," Clint said, "we'll just have to try our best not to."

Bledsoe entered the cantina and found Noah Bain having a bottle of whiskey for breakfast. The samurai sword was on the table in front of him.

The big man went to the bar and told the bartender, "Tequila." The man handed him a bottle. To each his own for breakfast. Bledsoe walked over and sat opposite Bain.

"So what are we gonna do with that sword?" he asked.

"What we're supposed to do with it," Bain said. "Deliver it to the buyer."

Bledsoe took a drink from the tequila bottle and said, "Still ain't gonna tell me who the buyer is?"

"It's not for you to know, Travis."

"Well then, answer me this," Bledsoe said. "You think your buyer will want to buy the girl, too?"

"No," Bain said, "he's not a slave trader."

"I tell ya," Bledsoe said, "I sure would like to get my hands on her. I ain't never been with a woman like that. Hell, it's been a long time since I been with a woman who *wasn't* a whore."

"You're not gonna touch her," Bain said.

"That a fact?"

"Yes, it is."

"So then you do have a buyer for her?" Bledsoe asked. "Or are we gonna sell her back to her old man?"

"Let's just say," Bain answered, "I've got plans."

"And you ain't gonna tell me about 'em?" Bledsoe asked. "Me? Your buddy?"

"If you'd left the girl behind, we wouldn't be havin' this problem about what to do with her. We were only after the sword."

"Well," Bledsoe said, "once the boys saw that house it was kinda hard to keep them from goin' through it, ya know? And then the girl turned up, and . . ."

"Yeah, yeah, forget it," Bain said. He stood up. "I'm goin' over to Betty's."

"Yeah, I guess I should go on over to the whorehouse," Bledsoe said. "Talkin' about that Connelly gal sure does stir the juices, don't it?"

Bain didn't answer. He left the cantina, but Bledsoe walked right along with him.

"Tell me somethin'," he said to Bain. "How's a homely fella like yerself get a pretty gal like that Betty? No offense intended. I wuz just wonderin'."

"Bledsoe," Bain said, "you push your luck, you know that?"

"Yeah, I know it, Noah," Bledsoe said, "but it's a great way to live, don't ya think?"

THIRTY

Around midday, Clint and Ki stopped to examine the trail.

"See it?" Ki asked.

"Yeah," Clint said. "They joined back up here and kept going west."

Ki stood in his stirrups and looked around.

"No sign of the sheriff or his deputy."

"They might have lost the trail," Clint said. "The sheriff's proven himself to be not much of a tracker."

"Or he lost them because he wanted to."

"If the sheriff's in with the gang, I feel bad for Sweet," Clint said.

"The kid could be dead," Ki said.

"I guess we'll just have to follow these tracks and find out."

"This is too easy," Ki said.

"I know what you mean," Clint said. "Once we picked the trail up again, it's been real easy to follow."

"A gang would only be this sloppy if they knew nobody was following them."

"And why would they think that?" Clint asked.

More and more it was beginning to look like the sheriff was not as bad a tracker as he appeared to be.

After about an hour, they reined in again and Ki got down to look the ground over.

"What do you see?"

"Could be one more horse than there was at the ranch," Ki said. "I can't be sure."

"So you're thinking it could be the sheriff?"

Ki mounted up.

"If it is, then this gang knows we're coming," he said.

"And if there's only one extra horse, then Sweet is dead," Clint said.

"I said I couldn't be sure."

"I know."

Clint looked at the ground. It was dry; there hadn't been any rain. Most of those tracks were days old, but somebody had recently trampled over them, and it was a lone rider, not two. Ki knew it, but wasn't saying. They were both probably hoping that Sweet was out there somewhere—maybe on foot, maybe trussed up, but hopefully alive.

Betty Holcomb stared at the ceiling while Noah Bain rutted, moaning in her ear. When he was finished and rolled off of her, she was determined not to let him fall asleep—not yet, anyway.

She pulled the sheet up to cover herself, then turned on her side and ran her hand over Bain's hairy chest.

"Noah?"

"Mmm?"

"I heard some of your men talking about leaving," she said.

"They don't make the decisions."

"But are you leavin' . . . soon?" she asked.

"Don't know for sure," Bain said sleepily. "Maybe."

"But you're gonna take me with you, right?" she asked.

"'Course," he mumbled. "Said I would, right?"

"Yes. You did say that," she responded.

He was asleep already, and it wasn't just the sex. He'd been drinking his breakfast again, and was dead drunk.

When he started snoring, she got up and went to the pitcher and basin. She poured some water into the basin, used a cloth to bathe herself. "A whore's bath," her friend Jessie called it, and Jessie should know.

She wondered if she could get Bain to give her some money so she could leave on her own and not have to count on him to keep his promise. Men made promises so easy, and they were so hard to keep, for some reason. Why not just not keep them, she wondered?

She dried off, but didn't want to go to the bed. It was damp with his sweat, and she had already slept all night. So she got dressed and very quietly left the room and the small house she owned on the edge of town.

She walked into town, which, though small, buzzed with activity early in the morning. She went to a small café to have some breakfast, wondering if Jessie was going to be able to join her, or if Bledsoe was also after a morning poke today.

THIRTY-ONE

Ki pointed at the signpost that said, "Serenity, twelve miles."

"Odd name for a town, if it's where they're holed up," he said.

"If they are there," Clint said, "they'll have somebody on watch."

"They've been sloppy so far," Ki pointed out.

"But we can't count on them to be that sloppy forever."

"Okay, so we circle, instead of riding right in," Ki said. "If the sheriff's with them they know we're coming, but they don't know when, or from what direction."

"They'll expect us to come this way," Clint said. "The main road."

"Plenty of tracks on this road," Ki said. "They could just be using it to mask theirs."

"Well, if they rode through this town and out the other end, like they did with that ghost town, we'll find out," Clint said. "But we better be careful going in, anyway."

"Agreed."

Ki started forward, but Clint put his hand on the man's arm to stop him.

"If we ride in and the gang is there," he said, "are you sure you don't want a gun?"

"I thought you were convinced," Ki said, taking a *Shuriken* out of his vest pocket.

"That was in a saloon," Clint said. "What about out in the street?"

Ki put away his throwing star and took a throwing knife from his sleeve.

"I use these at greater distances."

"Even the most accomplished knife thrower—" He stopped short when Ki's arms flashed; the knife flew through the air and struck a tree trunk about twenty feet away.

Ki rode over to the tree and reclaimed his knife.

"I see," Clint said.

Ki tucked the knife away in his sleeve again.

"Like you with your gun," he said, "I don't like to take out a knife or a star unless I'm going to use it."

"I understand. We better get moving. We want to take a look at this town before dark."

Bain woke in a bad mood, and with a headache. His mood worsened when he saw that Betty was not there. Still, since seeing Elizabeth Connelly, this girl had only been a small substitute. He no longer had any intention of taking Betty with him when he and his men moved on—if he, indeed, ever had intention of doing so.

In fact, it was probably time to go, anyway. They'd been in Serenity too long as it was, especially since it was only a few days from Chandlerville.

He got dressed quickly and went looking for his *segundo*, Bledsoe.

Bledsoe held Jessie's legs apart by the ankles and drove his rigid penis in and out of her with such force that she yelped out loud each time. In his mind, he was trying to split the girl in half. He'd paid for her; to him that meant he had the right to tear her in half if he wanted to.

But his mind wasn't really on Jessie today, so he just kept at her until he emptied into her, then released her legs and got off the bed.

"Is that all?" she asked, turning onto her back.

"For now," he said, pulling on his pants. "I've got some things to do, but maybe I'll be back later."

"I'll be waiting."

"Yeah," he said, "right, while you're fuckin' all your other johns you'll be waitin' for me."

She stretched and said, "Well, you're the . . . biggest."

He walked to the bed, rolled her over, and slapped her on each ass cheek. The resounding noise left two red welts in the shape of his hand.

"What was that for?" she demanded, rolling back.

"Marking my territory," he said. "I'll see you later, Jess."

She watched him walk out, then leaned over and rubbed both of her ass cheeks vigorously. She hoped the red would fade before her next client came up, but she doubted it.

Bledsoe came out of the whorehouse and saw Noah Bain coming toward him.

"Thought I'd find you here," Bain said.

"What's goin' on?"

"Get the men together at the cantina," Bain said.

"What for?"

"We're leavin'."

"When?"

"As soon as you get the men together," Bain said testily.

"What about the girl?"

"I'll bring her."

Bain turned to walk away but Bledsoe put a heavy hand on his arm.

"What's goin' on, Noah?"

"I just think it's time to leave, Travis," Bain said. "Have I been wrong before?"

"No, but—"

"Then do it. Okay?"

"Yeah, sure," Bledsoe said, dropping his hand. "Okay."

THIRTY-TWO

"Nobody watching," Clint said.

He and Ki dismounted and fell into a crouch. Below them were the lights of Serenity.

"That's wrong," Ki said. "Unless . . ."

"Unless what?"

Ki held up two fingers. "One of two things. One, they really are that careless. Two—"

"They're not there anymore."

"Right."

"No three? Maybe they want us to come in."

"I don't think they're stupid enough for a one, or a three," Ki said. "I think it's two."

"Why? I mean, why don't you think they're that stupid, or careless?"

"They've been operating with success for too long," Ki said. "They haven't been stupid up to now, and I don't think they'd have a sudden attack of it."

"So you say we should ride right in?" Clint asked.

"That's my suggestion," Ki said, "but I'm willing to go in first."

"Well, I do think you should go in first," Clint said, "but I'll be right behind you."

"How far?"

"Just far enough so that people don't think we're together."

"Plus I'll attract a lot of attention," Ki said. "It'll make you look . . . normal."

"Okay," Clint said, "go ahead and ride in. Get a hotel room. I'll follow and do the same."

"And then what?"

"We'll get some sleep; and in the morning, we'll find out if the gang is in town, or ever was in town."

"A good night's sleep in a bed," Ki said. "Sounds like a plan—that is, if we get to do it."

"If it's a trap, we'll find out soon enough."

"It's not a trap," Ki said.

"How can you be so sure?"

"If it was," Ki said, "we'd be fools to ride into it."

Clint waited, giving Ki an hour to ride in and get himself situated. He didn't see or hear anything that would indicate that the Japanese had any trouble.

Finally, he mounted Eclipse and rode into town himself.

Not knowing how many hotels were in town, they'd agreed to simply check into the first one they came to. While it was dark, it was not yet that late, so Clint was able to leave his horse at the livery before walking to the hotel.

"Second stranger in an hour," the old liveryman said. "I'm doin' good business."

"Pays to stay open after dark, old-timer."

"I guess so," the man said happily. "First fella was

funny-lookin', though. Looked Chinese, but wasn't. Also, his horse wasn't as handsome as yours."

"There are no horses as handsome as mine," Clint said.

"You got that right, friend."

Since the man was so talkative, Clint decided to press things.

"Riders going out, too, or just coming in?" he asked.

"Now how'd you know that?" the man asked. "We had about eight riders leave today."

"Eight?"

"Fellers who came in together a few weeks ago, decided to leave together, too."

"Weeks?" Clint asked.

"Maybe a month," the man said. "Then they up and left."

"When was that?"

"A few hours ago."

Damn, Clint thought. They had just missed them.

"So when will you be needing your horse?" the liveryman asked.

"Actually," Clint said, "I need him right now. Don't even unsaddle him."

"What?"

"I'm leaving town. Here." Clint paid the man, anyway. "And this is for the Japanese man's horse. Saddle him up."

"Japan—"

"Here," Clint said, giving the man more money. "Saddle it!"

"Yes, sir."

THIRTY-THREE

When Ki answered the door to his hotel room, he looked at Clint in surprise.

"Time to check out," Clint said.

"But I just checked in."

"They're gone," Clint said.

"So, can we get some sleep and then go after them?" Ki asked.

"No," Clint said, "they just left a few hours ago. We can't let them get any farther ahead of us."

"We can't track them at night," Ki said.

"We have an idea of the direction they went in," Clint said. "By morning, when it's light, we can pick up their trail."

"What if we go off the trail in the dark?"

"That's a chance I think we should take," Clint said, "just so they don't get much farther ahead of us. Three hours, Ki."

Ki stared at him.

"Look at you, all you've done is take off your hat."

"Yeah," Ki said, "yeah, okay. Let's go."

* * *

They were mounting up in front of the hotel when a dark-haired woman came up to them, holding a shawl tightly around herself.

"Are you the law?" she asked.

"Not exactly," Clint said. "We are part of a posse, though."

"Are you looking for Noah Bain and his men?"

Both men froze for a moment, then looked at her.

"What do you know about him?" Clint asked.

"Him and his gang were here for almost a month," she said. "Just left today."

"We know that much," Clint said.

"They got a woman with them."

"Do you know her name?"

"All I ever heard was a last name," she said. "Connelly."

Clint stepped up onto the boardwalk to stand in front of her. She was pretty, but had some hard, bitter lines in the corners of her mouth.

"Do you know anything else?" he asked.

"Somethin' about a sword?" she asked.

"Yes," Clint said, "A sword."

"Bain had a sword," she said. "Kept polishing it, lookin' at it."

"And the woman?" Clint asked. "How was she treated while they were here?"

"She wasn't here the whole month. Only about a week, I think. Nobody touched her, if that's what you mean," she said. "Don't know what was so special about her." She sniffed.

"When they rode out, was she on her own horse? Or riding double?"

"They gave her a horse of her own."

"And how many men were there?"

"Eight," she said. "I'm pretty sure there was eight, but you gotta worry about Bain and his man Bledsoe. They're the dangerous ones."

"Ma'am, you mind me asking why you're telling us all this?"

"Betty," she said, "my name's Betty. If they broke the law, they should pay. They kidnap that girl?"

"They did."

"Ain't right," she said, "ain't right at all."

As Clint mounted up, he had a feeling she was talking about something else, entirely.

THIRTY-FOUR

"You know," Ki said, "my horse isn't as surefooted as yours. We could have broke our necks."

"But you didn't."

"But we could have."

"It's daylight now," Clint said. "We're safe. In fact, we should push it now."

"Maybe your horse can push it," Ki said, "but mine needs some rest."

"Okay," Clint said, "let's pick up their trail, first. You can judge how far behind them we are, and then we'll rest a bit."

"A bit," Ki said, "my horse needs more than a bit."

"Maybe," Clint said, "you need fresh horse."

"Yeah," Ki said, "pull one out of your horse and I'll take it."

"I'll see what I can do."

At midday the following day, one of the men riding with Noah Bain and his gang called a halt to their progress.

"What is it?" Bain asked.

"What was the big hurry about leavin' Serenity that we had to do it and end up ridin' at night?"

"I just had a feelin' we should leave," Bain said. "And when I get a feelin', I go by it."

The man looked at Bledsoe, who nodded his head and said, "And he's usually right."

"But you don't have to ride much farther with us," Bain said.

"Why not?"

"Your part's done."

"I can't go back, Bain," the man said.

"I didn't say anythin' about you goin' back."

"Then wha—"

The man was caught completely off guard when Bledsoe sidled his horse up next to him and cut his throat from behind. The man's eyes widened, then he started to choke. Bledsoe gave him a shove and he fell off his horse, hitting the ground like a sack of wet cement.

Elizabeth Connelly caught her breath, then covered her mouth, but she was unable to look away.

Bain rode over to him and looked down.

"Thanks for your help . . . Sheriff."

They rode on, first slapping the sheriff's horse so that it took off in the opposite direction.

They picked up the trail near midday. Ki got down and studied it, then looked up at Clint.

"It's them, and we're still a few hours behind."

"Mount up, then."

Ki shook his head.

"You go ahead if you want, but my horse won't keep up with yours. Trying will just kill him."

"All right," Clint said, "okay. We'll give him an hour."

"Two," Ki said, "and that might not even do it."

"Okay, okay," Clint said, dismounting, giving in, "two."

After they took the saddles off their horses, they opened a couple of cans they'd taken from the bartender in Hardesty and started eating. They were almost done when they heard a horse approaching from ahead of them.

"Hear it?" Ki asked.

Clint's reply was to stand up. Ki followed. They waited as the horse came closer; it appeared riderless.

"Ho," Ki said, waving his hands, "easy, boy."

The horse slowed and allowed Ki to grab its reins.

"This is Sheriff Potts's horse," Clint said.

"You sure?" Ki studied it. "Yeah, you're right."

Clint ran his hand over the horse's neck, then its legs, finally moving back to the saddle.

"Blood here," Clint said.

"Fresh?"

"A few hours, I'd say."

"So he did catch up to them," Ki said.

"And they killed him, either because he caught up to them, or because they didn't need him anymore."

Clint looked at Ki.

"This horse is in better shape than yours."

"I'm not leaving my horse."

"I'm not suggesting that," Clint said. "I'm saying you can ride this one, and lead yours."

"Oh."

"We'll put your saddle on this one, leave the sheriff's saddle behind."

"Okay," Ki said, "that we can do."

"I better go through his saddlebags first," Clint said. "Who knows? Might find his badge."

"I'll switch saddles."

* * *

The sheriff's badge was not in his saddlebags. In fact, not much was. All Clint took from the saddle was the man's rifle. Never knew when you could use an extra gun.

They mounted up and looked at each other. They were both thinking the same thing: If the Sheriff was dead, what the hell had happened to the deputy?

THIRTY-FIVE

Three hours later, they came upon the sheriff's body. They both dismounted and Clint leaned over the man.

"Cut his throat," he said. "Don't think he ever knew what was coming."

He removed the man's badge, put it in his pocket. As a last thought, he took off the sheriff's gun belt and slung it over his saddle.

"We'll take the badge and his guns back to town when we're done," he said.

"We should bury him," Ki said.

"It'll put us further behind," Clint said.

"Maybe so," Ki said, "but it's what we should do."

Clint nodded. They looked around for a likely place, then dragged the body over. Next, they found some flat rocks they could use as shovels. They dug a shallow grave, rolled the man's body into it, and covered him up.

As they mounted up, Clint noticed that Ki was not holding the reins of his unsaddled horse.

"I've decided to leave him behind," Ki said. "I want to catch up to these bastards."

"So we push it?"

"We push it," Ki said. "I'll try my best to keep up with you."

They covered as much ground as they could, keeping to the pace of the slower horse. Clint knew Eclipse could run any other horse into the ground, and they weren't looking to do that.

"They must be pushing, too," Ki said. "We're not closing on them."

"We're not losing ground, either," Clint said. "I could push ahead of you, but when I caught up I'd be outnumbered eight to one, or worse."

"But if we catch up together it's not so bad?" Ki asked.

"Naw," Clint said. "Together we'd have them right where we want them."

Ki grinned and said, "Okay, let's just keep moving, then."

At dusk, Noah Bain put his hand up and called his men to a halt.

"We still got some time," Bledsoe said. "Won't be total dark for half an hour."

"The girl's tired," Bain said.

"So what?"

"She'll slow us down."

"That the real reason?" Bledsoe asked.

Bain gave him a hard look.

"The real reason is 'cause I said so, Travis," Bain said.

"Okay, okay," Bledsoe said, "you're the boss."

"Yeah," Bain said. "Remember that."

Bain had kept the girl close since they'd given her a horse of her own and kept the sword on his saddle.

Bledsoe was starting to worry that Bain thought both belonged to him.

They didn't belong to him; they belonged to the whole gang. Could be he was going to have to remind Noah Bain of that.

THIRTY-SIX

Clint and Ki decided to camp, rather than go on in the dark.

"They're ahead of us," Clint said. "Might as well not risk riding at night."

Ki agreed. They built a fire, made some coffee, and opened the last of the canned goods they had with them.

"We've never talked about your relationship with the girl's father," Ki said. "And the girl."

"Don Connelly and I saved each other's lives a few times some years back. As for Liz, I haven't seen her in twenty years. She was the prettiest little girl you'd ever want to see, and I guess she grew up well."

"Well enough for somebody to want to kidnap her at first sight," Ki said.

"The girl in town said nobody had touched her," Clint said. "I hope she's right."

"That woman looked pretty upset," Ki said. "I think maybe somebody promised to take her along when they left town and then ran out on her."

"That sounds about right," Clint said.

"First watch?" Ki asked.

"I'll take the first this time," Clint said. "You get some sleep."

"We'll catch up to them tomorrow," Ki said. "We better have a plan."

"We'll talk about it in the morning," Clint said. "We can both think it over tonight."

Ki nodded and wrapped himself up in his blanket and bedroll.

Clint and Ki weren't the only ones thinking. Noah Bain was having second thoughts about his gang, especially Bledsoe. If he could slip away with the girl and the sword, he could take the sword to the buyer, collect his money, and be pretty set for some time. Then he could decide what to do with Elizabeth Connelly. Selling her back to her father, or on the open market, could set him up for life.

All he had to do was figure out a way to get away from Bledsoe and the others. Which, considering all the snoring that was going on around him, might not be too hard.

There was only one man on watch.

Ki woke Clint in the morning and said, "We're out of coffee."

"That's fine," Clint said. "We've got to get going, anyway."

They saddled up and started riding.

Bledsoe woke that morning, rubbed his face with both hands, and noticed there was no coffee smell.

"Goddamnit, didn't I say there better be coffee—"

He started bellowing, but when he stood up and looked at the fire, he saw Duffy—the man on watch—prone on the ground.

"Jesus, Duffy, you fall asleep?" he demanded.

He got up, stomped over to the man, and nudged him with his toe. When Duffy didn't move, he bent over him and found that he wasn't asleep; he was unconscious.

"Goddamnit!" he said. He straightened up and looked around. "Wake up, goddamnit!"

The other men jerked awake—all but Noah Bain. He couldn't wake up because he wasn't there.

"Shit," he said. "Where's the girl?"

The men all glanced around as they got to their feet, shrugging or shaking their heads.

"Oh," Duffy moaned, at Bledsoe's feet.

"Wake up, Duffy," the big man said, kicking Duffy in the ribs. "What happened?"

"I dunno," Duffy said, holding his head and his ribs. "Somebody hit me."

"Yeah," Bledsoe said, "somebody. Goddamn Bain, he took off with the girl and—I'll bet—the sword!"

Bledsoe stormed around camp, but there was no sight of the girl or the sword.

"Who does he think he is?" he demanded aloud. "I'll kill 'im."

"What do we do, Travis?" somebody asked.

"Get mounted, damn it!" Bledsoe said. "We're gonna find him, the girl, and the sword, and I'm gonna kill the two of them!"

THIRTY-SEVEN

Clint and Ki rode into the cold camp, looked around without dismounting.

"Nine people," Ki said.

"Looks like they left in a hurry," Clint said. "The fire's still smoldering."

"Maybe they felt us coming," Ki said. "If that fire's still warm, then we're closing in."

"Wait," Clint said. "Listen."

Ki quieted down and obeyed.

"Horses," he said, "sounds like two of them."

"Let's take cover," Clint said.

They rode over behind a stand of rocks large enough to hide behind and dismounted.

"Can't be the gang," Ki said. "These riders are coming from behind us."

"Maybe some of them doubled back," Clint said. "We'll know in the next few minutes."

They waited and watched . . . and suddenly two riders came into view, their horses' hooves loud on the hard ground.

"Stop right there!" Clint said, stepping out into the open.

"Mr. Adams!" Eddie Castro said. "Jesus, am I glad it's you."

"Castro," Clint said.

Ki stepped out, shaking his head.

"And Deputy Sweet," he said. "Where have you been?"

"Almost dead," Sweet said. His clothes were a mess, and he had multiple scratches on his face and hands—probably elsewhere, too.

"Dismount, boys," Clint said.

Both men stepped down, Sweet having to steady himself as he did so.

"You okay?" Clint asked.

"Just about," Sweet said.

"What happened to you?"

"The sheriff tried to kill me," Sweet said. "We was riding along, and suddenly he pushed me off my horse. I went over a cliff. When I woke up, I was surprised that I wasn't dead—even though I felt pretty bad."

"And how did the two of you hook up?" Clint asked. "I sent Castro back to town."

"I never went back. I tried to follow some tracks I saw on the ground, and I ended up meeting up with Deputy Sweet."

"I was on foot," Sweet said, "but Castro rode down my horse and then we had to decide whether to keep going, or go back."

"And you kept coming," Clint said.

"Well," Sweet said, "I am the law, and I had to tell you that the sheriff was crooked."

"The sheriff is also dead," Clint said. "Apparently his partners decided they didn't need him anymore."

"I guess that puts me in charge," Sweet said.

"How do you figure?" Ki asked.

Sweet tapped his badge.

Clint laughed. "You've grown up a lot in the past few days, huh?"

"Grow up or die, right?" Sweet asked.

"Okay, Deputy," Clint said, "what do you want to do?"

"What have we got?"

Clint explained how they found the town of Serenity, but the gang had left a few hours before. They'd been on their trail ever since.

"So now, when we catch up to them," Sweet said, "there'll be four of us, not two."

The three men looked at Castro.

"I don't have a gun."

Clint walked to his horse, removed the sheriff's holster and rifle, and handed them to Castro.

"Don't shoot any of us," he said.

Castro strapped on the pistol and slid the rifle into his saddle scabbard.

"I'll do my best," he said.

"How far behind are we?" Sweet asked.

"Couple of hours, maybe," Ki said. "We found their camp with the fire still smoldering."

"Then we're wasting time," Sweet said. "We better get movin'."

They all mounted up and Sweet said, "I can't track very well."

"I'll take the lead," Ki said.

Clint nodded.

"But when we catch them, I'm in charge," Sweet said. "I know I'm inexperienced, but I got the badge and I got to do my job."

"Understood," Clint said, "Deputy."

THIRTY-EIGHT

Travis Bledsoe knew he had six nervous men riding behind him. They had been following Noah Bain for months, and now he was gone. They had followed Bledsoe into many bloodbaths, but it had always been Bain who did the planning.

Duffy rode up alongside Bledsoe.

"What?" Bledsoe asked.

"The men wanna know what's goin' on," Duffy said. "Where's Bain goin'?"

"That's what we're gonna find out," Bledsoe said, "by followin' him."

"He can't be runnin' out on us," Duffy said, "not after all this time."

"Why not?" Bledsoe said.

"We pulled lots of jobs together, Travis. He never did nothin' like this before.

"Maybe he never found nothin' he wanted for himself before."

"You gonna kill 'im?"

"I said I was, didn't I?"

"And the sword?" Duffy asked.

"We'll find a buyer," Bledsoe said. "As soon as we catch Bain, and I kill him."

"But—"

"But what?" Bledsoe said. "He ran out on us, Duffy. Go back and tell that to the men."

"So you're in charge?" Duffy asked.

"Somebody's got to be," Bledsoe said. "You want the job?"

"Not me."

"Then go back and tell 'em, Duffy," Bledsoe said. "I don't want to kill any of you, so get 'em all to do as I say. Got it?"

"I got it, Travis."

Duffy fell back.

Bledsoe wondered how he could get away from all the men, find Bain, and take the girl and the sword for himself. It wouldn't be so easy, since the men had been run out on once, already.

"Why did you take me with you?" Elizabeth asked Noah Bain.

"Would you rather have stayed with them?" he asked. "Bledsoe and the rest?"

They were riding side by side, and she had still made no attempt to escape.

"I still want my chance to kill Bledsoe," she said.

"And me?"

"Him first," she said. "He killed my mother."

"I never told him to kill anybody," Bain said. "I just want you to know that."

"But she's dead, anyway," Liz said. "And so are other people. It didn't have to happen."

"I told him not to make a mess."

"Is that what you call killing people?" she asked. "Making a mess?"

"That's what killin' people is, missy," Bain said. "Makin' a helluva mess."

"Well then, I guess I'll wait for my chance to make a mess."

Bain turned his head and looked at her profile. She was sitting tall in the saddle, ramrod straight, her chin up.

"You ain't scared?"

She looked at him and he saw nothing in her eyes.

"Of course I'm scared," she said. "I kept waiting for one of your idiots to come in and rape me, if you didn't come in first."

"And Bledsoe? Were you waitin' for him?"

"I was hopin' he'd come in and try to rape me," she said. "I want to kill him with my bare hands."

"And you think you could?"

She turned her head to face forward again.

"Or die trying," she said.

"You're somethin' real special, ain't you?" Bain asked.

"What would you know about that?" she asked. "What about the sword? Why did you steal the sword?"

"The sword is what we were after," Bain said. "Bledsoe had orders to get the sword, and that was it. Everything else he did on his own."

"Makes no difference to me," she said. "I'd kill all of you, if I could."

"Well, maybe you'll still get your chance," he said, "because those boys are not just gonna give up because I left."

"They'll come after you?"

"Bledsoe will," Bain said. "The others will have to decide if they want to follow him or not."

"What about the posse?" she asked. "And my father?"

"They won't find us."

"So what will you do with me, and the sword?"

"I have a buyer for the sword," Bain said.

"And me?"

"I still haven't decided what to do with you," he said.

"Do you want me for yourself?" she asked.

He looked at her.

"You're a virgin, aren't you?" he asked.

"What makes you say that?"

"You're just so . . . fresh, and clean."

"So?"

"Would you come to bed with me—soil yourself—just for a chance to kill me?"

She looked at him and said, "Oh, yes."

THIRTY-NINE

"What kind of a girl is Elizabeth?" Clint asked Castro, as the four of them rode together. Sweet rode ahead with Ki, trying to learn what he could about tracking.

"She's beautiful," Castro said. "She's more—"

"I'm not concerned with how she looks," Clint said, cutting him off. "What kind of person is she? How is she going to be reacting through all this?"

"Oh," Castro said, blinking, "well . . . she's spunky. I think the men who took her better not turn their backs on her. They killed her mother, and she's gonna want revenge."

"Oh great," Clint said, "that'd be a perfect way to get herself killed."

"Oh," Castro said, "she's much too beautiful to kill, Mr. Adams."

"Yeah, well, I don't know if these kinds of men are going to care about that."

"Any man would," Castro said.

"Well," Clint said, "let's hope you're right."

* * *

Later in the day, Sweet and Castro changed places, and Clint decided to ask Sweet the same question.

"How much do you know about Elizabeth Connelly, Deputy?"

"Um, well, I ain't never had no personal time with her, but . . . she sure is beautiful—"

"What kind of person is she?" Clint asked. "How is she going to react to this kidnapping, and the killing of her mother?"

"Well," Sweet said, "if I was in this gang I wouldn't wanna turn my back on her. She'd stick a knife in the man who killed her mother, given half a chance."

"They'd kill her if she did that," Clint said.

"Well . . . I can't imagine any man killing Miss Elizabeth, Mr. Adams," Sweet said.

"Why not?"

"She's just too damn beautiful."

Well, if every member of the gang fell in love with her, he thought, that just might keep her safe.

But he wouldn't want to bet his—or her—life on it.

"They stopped here," Ki said, some time later. "Milled about some."

"They may be at odds with each other," Clint said. "May be fighting."

"About what?" Sweet asked.

"Money," Ki said, "the girl . . . wait a minute."

Ki dismounted, got down on one knee.

"What is it?"

"I'm seeing two less horses, here," he said.

"They split up here?"

"No, no," Ki said, walking back, "I should've seen it before. They're down two horses. They rode in here with two less. Probably left camp that way."

"A falling-out," Clint said. "Somebody might have left with the sword."

"Or the girl," Ki said.

"Or both," Sweet said.

"Should we go back and pick up their trail?" Castro asked.

"No," Ki said, "I think the rest of them are already tracking them, trampling their trail. We just have to keep following them."

"Well," Clint said, "if that's what we have to do, we better get to it."

FORTY

"Where are we going?" Elizabeth asked.

Bain looked at her. She was riding next to him, hands very free, and she obviously knew how to ride. If she bolted, he'd have to shoot her to stop her, because he probably wouldn't catch her. But she hadn't tried to escape. Not once. Maybe she was serious about wanting to kill him and Travis.

"Why do you want to know now?" he asked. "You haven't asked all day."

"It's going to be dark soon," she said. "Are we going to get where we're going before dark?"

"No," he said. "We'll have to camp."

"Aren't you afraid the others will catch up?"

"No," he said. "They're a bunch of idiots. They won't know what to do, or what direction to go."

"Is that true of Bledsoe, too?"

"No," he said, "Travis will probably catch up."

"And?"

"And I'll have to kill him."

"Or he'll kill you."

"What do you care?" he asked. "That'll make one less for you to kill."

"No, you're right," she said. "I'll enjoy watching the two of you try to kill each other."

They rode in silence for a while after that, until she asked another question. "Who's the buyer?"

"What?"

"The buyer for the sword," she said. "Who is it?"

"Why does that matter to you?"

"I'm just making conversation," she said. "But also, I'm curious."

"Why?" he asked. "Will you wanna kill that person, too? After all, he paid for us to go to your ranch."

"You're right," she said. "I never thought of that. I suppose I will have to kill him, too."

"Have you ever killed anyone?" he asked. "Or even seen anyone killed?"

"No," she said, "but I'm willing to start now."

"We gotta camp, Travis," Duffy said. "The men are tired."

"I'm not stopping," Bledsoe said. "I'm gonna catch up with them."

"At night?" Duffy asked. "You'll break your horse's leg—or your neck."

Bledsoe turned his head and looked at Duffy, then turned to look at the men riding behind him.

"You and the men go ahead and camp, and then catch up," Bledsoe suggested. "By the time you do, I'll have caught up to them and taken care of them. I'll have the sword."

"That stupid sword," Duffy said. "We got a lot of other stuff outta that house, you know. Valuable stuff. We made out good. What's so special about that sword?"

"It's special to somebody," Bledsoe said. "Noah had a buyer."

"And do you know who the buyer is?"

"No."

"How you gonna sell it then?"

"He'll tell me who the buyer is," Bledsoe said, "before I kill him."

"Are you sure?"

Bledsoe looked at Duffy and grinned tightly.

"Dead sure."

"And you're gonna share with us after you sell it?" Duffy asked.

"'Course I will, Duffy," Bledsoe said. "You don't think I'd run out on all of you, like Noah did to us, do ya?"

"No, Travis," Duffy said, "no, I don't think so."

"You go ahead and tell the men to stop and camp," Bledsoe said. "By the time you all catch up, I'll have everything we need: the sword, and the girl."

"If we go on after dark," Ki said, "we'll catch up to them."

"If they camp," Sweet said.

"They'll camp."

"What makes you think so?" Sweet asked.

"Because they're either stupid, or arrogant."

"But if they're after the ones who left," Castro asked, "wouldn't they keep goin'?"

"I'm thinking," Clint said, "that the man who left is probably the brains, the one who knows who the buyer for the sword is. And he probably took the girl."

"All the more reason they'll be chasin' him," Sweet said.

"They'll be chasing their tails," Clint said. "Without a leader they won't know which way to turn."

"Like a chicken without a head," Ki said.

"Exactly."

"Then what good is capturing them?" Sweet asked. "We want the leader. Noah Bain."

"We'll catch him," Clint said. "Travis Bledsoe will probably lead us to him. But let's start at the bottom. Ki will take the lead, and we'll follow single file. Agreed?"

They all agreed.

Ki came up to Clint before the men headed out.

"Two horses left that camp," he said. "What if it's Bain and Bledsoe? With the girl riding double?"

"Why don't we cross that bridge when we come to it?" Clint asked.

FORTY-ONE

"We go from here on foot," Ki said, holding his hand up two hours later.

"Why?" Sweet asked.

"Because," Ki said, "they're camped just ahead. Can't you smell it?"

Sweet sniffed the air, as did Castro.

"Coffee?" Sweet asked.

"Bacon?" Castro said hopefully.

"Smoke," Clint said, "just smoke. We're upwind of them, but I can still smell their fire."

"If they're making coffee or bacon or whatever, we can't smell it, yet," Ki said, "but they're up ahead."

They secured their horses and moved ahead on foot.

Duffy sat at the fire, putting on a fresh pot of coffee. The men were complaining that all they had to eat was beef jerky. Whatever bacon or beans had been left, Bain had taken along with the sword and the girl. Duffy didn't know what to do about it. He wasn't a leader. None of them were. Bain was the leader, and Bain was gone.

Bledsoe was their leader when they were on a job, but he never made any plans. And now he was gone, too, chasing after Bain.

Duffy and the others did what they were told, or acted out of reflex, but never planned their actions. They just weren't smart enough.

They were milling about camp, not doing anything together. It was like they were lost. Duffy was only making coffee because he wanted coffee.

"What are we supposed to do?" one of the man asked him. His name was Larch, and he hunkered down next to Duffy. "Wait here for Bledsoe to come back?"

"No, he wanted us to continue on in the mornin'," Duffy said. "Follow his trail."

"Yeah, but, what are we gonna do without Noah?" Larch asked. "He's always been in charge."

"I don't know, Larch," Duffy said. "How would I know?"

He reached for the coffeepot and burned his hand.

"Shh," Ki said. "Wait here."

They waited while he went ahead. He came back and nodded.

"They're camped just ahead."

"How many?" Clint asked.

"Looks like six."

"No Bain, no Bledsoe, I'll bet," Clint said.

"They ran out on them?" Castro asked.

"Probably," Clint said. "I don't know how much that sword is worth, but it must be enough."

"Elizabeth is worth more than the sword," Castro said.

"I agree," Sweet said. "If Bain and Bledsoe have her, we should bypass these men and go after them."

"These men broke the law," Clint said. "They killed people at the Connelly ranch. And you're the law."

"You have to do your job," Ki said. "You can't just decide what part to do and what part not to do."

"But Elizabeth—" Castro started.

"No," Sweet said, "they're right. We have to take them."

"Let's go," Ki said. "We can catch them in a cross fire."

"Wait," Clint said.

He took the deputy's badge off Sweet's shirt, then took out the sheriff's star and pinned it on.

"Okay," he said, "now we can go."

FORTY-TWO

They moved in close to the camp, then broke off into twos. Ki and Sweet went one way, Clint and Castro went the other.

"You don't fire unless I do," Clint told the kid, "or they do, understand?"

"Yes, sir."

Castro looked scared out of his wits, and he was sweating heavily.

"Just take it easy," Clint said. "It'll be okay. Take a deep breath."

"Yes, sir." He did.

"Okay," Clint said and looked over at the camp.

There was a fire going and two men were hunkered down by it; the other four were spread out. Two were lying down, one was sitting, and the other was pacing. They looked like what they were: men without a leader.

"In the camp," Sweet's voice called out. "This is acting sheriff Hal Sweet. Throw down your guns and put your hands up."

* * *

If they'd had a leader, maybe they would have dropped their guns. But they didn't; all they had was their reflexes, which led them to draw their guns and start firing into the darkness.

Clint's mistake had been in telling Castro not to fire unless the men did. They were firing into the dark and not coming anywhere near hitting anybody, but Castro panicked and started firing back. He didn't hit anyone, but the flashes from his gun gave the men in the camp something to fire at. The boy went down in a hail of bullets, and Clint hit the ground.

"Crap," Ki said.

Sweet started firing.

The men in the camp turned toward the new shots and returned fire.

Ki ducked down and moved closer. He was within range with his *Shuriken* and knives. They all went straight and true.

When the outlaws began firing toward Sweet and Ki, Clint stood up and calmly fired. He was angry that Castro was down, and probably dead. He picked up Castro's gun and fired with both hands. Every chunk of lead he sent into camp struck a man.

Then it was quiet.

"Clint?" Ki yelled. "You hit?"

"No," Clint called back, "but Castro's down."

"Dead?"

Clint leaned over the boy and checked him.

"Yeah, damnit. Sweet?"

"I'm okay."

"Let's move in!" Clint said.

They moved slowly into camp, Ki walking behind Clint and Sweet because they had their guns out. Ki leaned over the first man he came to and retrieved one of his knives.

Clint and Sweet checked the other men.

"All dead," Clint said. "Damn it. That kid started firing. He panicked—"

"It wasn't your fault," Ki said, pulling a knife from another of the dead men's possessions.

"I should've kept control of him," Clint said. "Now he's dead, and they're all dead and we've got nobody to question."

Ki walked around the camp, came back to the fire where Clint and Sweet were standing.

"I don't see anybody fitting the description of Bain or Bledsoe, and the girl's not here."

"Okay," Clint said, "so we figured something right. Either Bain and Bledsoe left with the girl . . ."

". . . or one of them left with the girl and the other is following."

"And this is probably what they wanted," Clint said, waving his hand. "The rest of these men gone."

"Well," Sweet said, "we obliged 'em. What now?"

"I'll go get the horses," Ki said. "We'll spend the rest of the night here."

"Sweet and I will move the bodies," Clint said. "In the morning, we'll bury the kid and move on."

"We ain't buryin' the others?" Sweet asked.

"That'll take too long," Clint said. "No, we'll bury the kid and then keep going."

Ki slipped into the darkness to go and fetch the horses.

FORTY-THREE

Bain heard him coming from a mile off. Bledsoe was such a big man, there was no way he could walk soft.

"What is it?" Elizabeth asked, seeing the look on Bain's face.

"Travis must have ridden all night," he said. "He's out there now."

"Where?" She started to turn her head.

"Don't look around!" Bain snapped. "You have to make a choice now, lady: him or me."

"A choice?"

"He's gonna kill me, today, or I'm gonna kill him," he said. "It's up to you."

"Why me?"

"Because you can help me now, or you can give me up to him. Let him know that I hear him comin'."

"I see."

"But you have to decide now."

She hesitated, then said, "What do I have to do?"

"Nothin'," he said. "Just sit there and don't let on we know he's comin'."

"You mean, act as bait?"

"Well," Bain said, "you can be my bait, or his meat."

Bledsoe tied off his horse and continued on foot. He could smell their camp. When he got even closer, he thought he could smell the girl.

As he moved in closer, he drew his gun. They were probably getting ready to break camp, saddle the horses, and get going. Bain was smart enough to be on watch, but he couldn't count on the girl for anything. He'd be tired from being up all night, and could get careless.

He stepped as lightly as he could as he worked his way toward the camp. The girl was sitting at the fire. Bledsoe could see the two unsaddled horses, but Noah Bain was nowhere in sight.

The girl was just sitting there, pretty as you please, and he noticed that her hands were not tied, and neither were her feet.

What the hell, he thought?

Elizabeth was frightened.

She'd been scared the whole time, but tried her best not to show it. Now, however, she was caught between two madmen, and who knew what could happen? In trying to kill each other they could kill her by mistake.

Still, her chances of killing both of these men were slim. But if one of them killed the other one, then her chances of killing the one left standing improved.

She sat still in front of the fire, wondering which of these men she'd be in more danger with. Which one would she have a better chance of killing? Her final decision was Bain. Bledsoe was an animal; at least Bain had some brains. He wouldn't hurt her as long as he thought he could make money from her.

Bledsoe was not as smart as Bain, and if she ended up with him there was more of a chance of being brutalized by him.

So she sat as still as Bain had told her, and hoped that he would be able to outsmart Bledsoe and kill him.

FORTY-FOUR

Clint, Ki, and Sweet buried young Eddie Castro and stood over his grave.

"Somebody should say somethin'," Sweet said.

Clint and Ki exchanged a glance.

"Sorry, kid," Clint said, finally, "but you're in a better place now. At least, that's what all the religions say."

"You ain't religious, Mr. Adams?" Sweet asked.

"Not much."

Sweet looked at Ki.

"Do you follow any religion?"

"Not in this country," Ki said.

They all put their hats back on and walked to their horses. Ki had decided to leave behind both his horse and the sheriff's, and he switched to Castro's mount. They passed the bodies of the outlaws, stacked like cordwood.

"We should bury them, too," Sweet said, as they rode past.

"No time, Sweet," Clint said. "If you want, you can come back and do it later."

"Maybe we could all do it, on the way back," he said.

"Yeah," Ki said, "maybe."

It was almost eleven a.m. when they came across the camp with the body in it.

"Wait," Clint said, as acting sheriff Sweet started to ride on ahead.

"What?"

"Could be a trap," Ki said.

"I'll go in," Clint said. "Cover me."

Ki directed Sweet to fan out to one side while he covered from the other. When they were in position, Clint dismounted and walked into the camp, gun in hand. Ki had a *Shuriken* in each hand, while Sweet was holding his gun ready.

Clint entered the camp, saw the gray ash of the campfire. There were no horses in camp, although he could see where they had been picketed. All he could figure was that one man had made camp with the girl, and the other man had found them. In the ensuing exchange, one of them ended up dead.

He walked over to the body and used the toe of his boot to turn him over, although it really wasn't necessary. Just from the sheer size of the man he knew it was Travis Bledsoe. Noah Bain had obviously gotten the best of the big man.

He turned and waved to Ki and Sweet to come on in.

"It's Bledsoe," Clint said, "unless there's another member of that gang who fits this description."

"Must have come into camp on foot," Ki said. "Let me find his horse."

"Be careful," Clint said.

Ki nodded and left camp.

"Go through his pockets, see what you find," Clint said.

"Why me?" Sweet asked.

"Because you're the acting sheriff," Clint said.

The young man got down on one knee and quickly went through the dead man's pockets, then stood up.

"Nothin'."

"Too bad. Let's see what Ki finds."

"If this is Bledsoe, then Bain has Elizabeth," Sweet said.

"Bain is the brains of the gang," Clint said. "She's safe as long as he thinks he can make money off of her."

"Or if he wants her for himself."

"I don't think a hardened gang leader is going to fall in love in the job, Sweet."

"You haven't seen her," Sweet said.

Clint shook his head. Young men in love could hardly think of anything else.

Ki came back into camp leading a big dun.

"Sure is big enough to be his horse," Clint said, although the horse didn't have the sheer size of Eclipse.

They went through the saddlebags, found a letter addressed to Travis Bledsoe.

"Postmark is from months ago, somewhere in Texas," Ki said. "Believe it or not, it's from his mother."

"Okay," Clint said, "it's Bledsoe's horse, and the dead man is Bledsoe. So now we're tracking Noah Bain."

Ki studied the ground.

"Two horses, still heading west," he said.

"The girl is riding her own horse," Clint said. "That'll slow him down."

"She's an expert rider," Sweet said.

"She might be," Clint said, "and if she is, she'll be able to slow him down even more."

"We got plenty of light," Ki said. "We should be able to catch up today, if we ride hard."

"Then we'll ride hard," Clint said.

Ki patted the neck of Bledsoe's big horse and said, "I'm going to switch mounts again."

"I don't blame you," Clint said. "That horse would have the best chance of keeping up with Eclipse."

Ki switched his saddle over to the dun, cinched it in tight, and mounted.

"You gonna go ahead of us, Clint?" Sweet asked.

"No," Clint said, "we'll ride hard, but we'll stay together—unless one of us has to stop. Then the others go on without him."

"I ain't stoppin'," Sweet said. "I'll go on foot, if I have to."

Clint doubted that Sweet's mount would be able to keep up to Ki's new mount and Eclipse, so the young acting sheriff might very well end up on foot.

FORTY-FIVE

Elizabeth had been surprised at how easily Bain had killed Bledsoe. One minute she was sitting by the fire and the next Bain had been pushing Bledsoe ahead of him into camp, having already disarmed him.

"He was standing out there starin' at you," he had said. "It was easy for me to creep up behind him."

"You ain't gonna get away with this, Noah," Bledsoe had said. "The other men are comin' after you, too."

"You're kiddin', right?" Bain had asked. "Without somebody to lead them, that bunch will be goin' in circles for months. That is, if a posse don't catch up to them first."

"So what're you plannin' to do?" Bledsoe asked. "Sell the sword and keep the girl?"

"You're not gonna have to worry about that, Travis," Bain said. "You'll be dead."

"Nah," Bledsoe said, "if you was gonna kill me, you woulda shot me in the back by now. Now it's too late. I'm gonna take your gun away and feed it to you."

She'd been shocked when Bledsoe turned around to

face Bain, and even more shocked when Bain pumped three bullets into the big man. Bledsoe fell to the ground and didn't move.

"He was right," he then told her. "Normally I woulda shot him in the back."

"Why didn't you?" she asked.

"Because I wanted you to see me kill him," Bain said. "I wanted you to see your first dead man."

"Did you think it would scare me?" she'd asked.

"I don't know," he said, "maybe I thought it would excite you."

They'd saddled up then and rode out, heading southwest, and it was later in the day that she saw the signpost for El Paso.

Now she asked, "Are we going to El Paso?"

"You ever been there?"

"No."

"Use to be kind of wild, but it ain't so much, anymore."

"Is that where you're selling the sword, or me?" she asked.

"I don't know," he said. "I guess we'll just have to see, won't we?"

"El Paso," Clint said.

"You're probably right," Ki said.

"That's where you think he's goin'?" Sweet asked.

"Where else makes sense?" Clint asked. "He can sell the sword—and the girl—and then go into Mexico."

"Or take the girl with him to Mexico," Ki said. "Use her up and then sell her."

"Stop!" Sweet said.

They both looked at him.

"We can't let him do that!"

"We have to take a chance," Clint said. "Split up. Two of us stay on his trail, and one of us can cut southwest, try to get between him and El Paso."

"*If* he's goin' to El Paso," Sweet said.

Clint shrugged.

"If he's not," he said, "then one of us will be out of it. The other two will probably catch him—maybe before he gets to El Paso."

"I'll go," Ki said.

"No, I'll go," Clint said. "It was my idea. Besides, I know a shortcut."

"You knew where he was going all along," Ki accused.

"No," Clint said, "just a little while ago. I realized where we were, and I know I can get ahead of him."

"*If* he's goin' to El Paso," Sweet said again.

"Don't worry, Sheriff," Clint said, "if he's not, you and Ki will catch him."

"B-but," Sweet said, pointing at Ki, "he doesn't even wear a gun."

"Don't worry," Clint said, "you do."

FORTY-SIX

"Who's the buyer?" Elizabeth asked. She eyed the sword, which hung from Bain's saddle horn.

"What do you care?"

"Well, whoever it is, he's the reason you came to my house and killed my mother. I'd like to know."

"I think I'll keep that to myself until we get to El Paso," Bain said. "If you don't mind."

"Can I see the sword?"

He turned his head and smiled at her. It was an ugly smile.

"It's sharp," he said. "You'll cut yourself."

They rode in silence from that point on until, about five miles outside of El Paso, they saw a rider up ahead.

Clint spotted the two riders, a man and a woman. The man was thick-set and squat, while the girl sat straight and tall on her horse.

He decided to get ahead of them. He had a good half-mile on the pair when he took up position in the road and waited.

* * *

Bain reined in, told Elizabeth to do the same.

"Who is it?" she asked. "The man you're supposed to meet?"

"No," Bain said, "we're supposed to meet in town."

"Why isn't he moving?" she asked.

"I don't know."

"What are we going to do?"

Bain pulled his gun and pointed it at Elizabeth.

"Wha—"

"Just keep quiet and ride slowly."

He took the reins in his left hand, kept the gun trained on Elizabeth, and they rode forward.

As the two riders got closer, Clint saw that Bain had his gun pointed at Elizabeth. Also, as they got closer, he saw why all the young men he'd met were in love with her. She was truly a beauty. He knew she had to be scared, but she didn't show it.

He was impressed.

"Hold it," Clint said, when they came within fifteen feet of him.

"You see me with a gun on the girl?" Bain asked.

"I see."

"Who are you?"

"Are you all right, Liz?" he asked.

"I-I'm fine."

"I said, who are you?" Bain said.

"My name's Clint Adams," Clint said.

"Clint?" Elizabeth said, looking surprised.

"Your dad sent me to get you, Liz."

"Oh my God, it is you," she said.

"Adams?" Bain asked. "The Gunsmith?"

"That's right."

"Why'd he send you?"

"He and I are old friends."

Bain didn't look happy. That was good. The man was agitated.

"Didn't plan on that, did you?" Clint asked.

"Just drop your gun and get out of the way," Bain said.

"I can't do that," Clint said. "It's Bain, right? It must be, because we found Bledsoe dead."

"Yeah, I'm Bain. I killed Bledsoe, and I'll kill this girl if you don't drop your gun and move out of the way."

"No," Clint said. "If I drop my gun, you'll kill me, because if you leave me alive I'll come after you. So it doesn't do me any good to drop my gun."

"I'll kill 'er!"

"I'll bet I can draw and fire before you can pull the trigger."

Clint saw Elizabeth shift in the saddle. It was a move Bain didn't see because he was looking at Clint.

"You wanna bet her life on that?"

"You want to bet *your* life?"

Bain firmed his jaw, getting angrier and angrier.

"If you kill her," Clint said, "I kill you. Your best bet is to drop it."

"Goddamnit—"

Suddenly, Elizabeth fell off her horse—just slid from her saddle to the ground on her right side, between her and Bain.

"What the—" Bain said, taking his eyes off Clint.

Clint drew and fired. The bullet hit Bain high on the right shoulder, causing him to drop his gun. It didn't knock him from his saddle, though. That happened when Elizabeth grabbed the sword and ran it right through him with a scream.

FORTY-SEVEN

"I had to kill him," Elizabeth said.

"I understand," Clint said.

"I said I was going to," she went on. "I practically promised him that I was going to kill him. So I had to do it."

Clint nodded.

"It's okay, baby," Donald Connelly said. He put his arm around her and hugged her. "It's okay."

They were sitting on a sofa in their house. They had both gone back to the house at the same time.

"Can she do that?" Sweet asked.

Clint and Ki looked at acting sheriff Sweet.

"I mean, do I have to arrest her for killin' him?" he asked.

"No," Clint said. "She did it in El Paso, and she did it in self-defense."

"But you shot Bain," Sweet said. "He had dropped his gun—"

"Did he?" Clint asked. "Were you there?"

"No, but—"

"I was there," Clint said, "and I said it was self-defense. So the sheriff in El Paso didn't arrest her, you don't have to, either."

"Thank you all for bringing her back to me," Connelly said. He gave Clint a look that said a private thank you, as well.

"That's okay, Donny," Clint said.

"Yes, thank you all," she said. She got up, gave Ki and Sweet a kiss on the cheek, and then gave Clint a big hug and a kiss. Sweet's face turned red.

"We'd better go," Clint said, "and let the two of you be alone."

"Will you be leaving town?" Connelly asked.

"Tomorrow," Clint said. "I'm going to leave tomorrow."

"We'll have a drink first," Connelly said.

"Sure."

Clint, Ki, and Sweet left the Connelly house, and stopped outside by their horses.

"I'm leaving now," Ki said, "right from here."

"Not staying for the presentation?" Clint asked. "I understand Mr. Tanaka is coming in tomorrow."

"Are you staying to meet him?" Ki asked.

"No."

"Why not?"

"My job is over."

"So's mine," Ki said. He shook hands with Clint, and then Sweet, then mounted up and rode off.

"What about the buyer?" Sweet asked Clint. "Don't we have to find the buyer?"

"It would be nice if we could," Clint said, "but Bain's dead, and he's the only one who knew who the buyer was."

"But . . . what if they try to steal it again?"

"If they do, it'll have to be from Mr. Tanaka," Clint said, "and probably from Japan."

"But . . . they could try tonight."

Clint slapped Sweet on the shoulder and said, "That's your worry, acting sheriff. That's your worry."

Watch for

LADY EIGHT BALL

346th novel in the exciting GUNSMITH series
from Jove

Coming in October!